THE TEARS IN THE WATER

A Pale Woods Suspense

Courtnee Turner Hoyle

Pale Woods Publishing

The Tears in the Water

A Pale Woods Suspense

Copyright © November 21, 2023

Erwin, TN

by Courtnee Turner Hoyle

Library of Congress Control Number: 2023921979

Print IBSN: 979-8-9876468-9-2

E-book ISBN: 979-8-9876468-7-8

Cover Design: Taylor Dawn, Sweet15 Designs, LLC

To my mama,
you loved this book, and I'm glad you couldn't figure it out

To Legacee, it may be a "wild world", but you are definitely "good"

To my fellow introverts and ambiverts,
don't let your loneliness or empathy guide your romantic decisions

More of Courtnee's Titles

Paranormal Mystery

My Brother's Keeper

Pinky Swear

Rose Colored Glasses

Romance

Finding Emma

Finding David

Paranormal Suspense

Solomon's Tears

Thriller

Hollis's Hobby

Fantasy

Cascade

Under Archard's Dome

Middle-Grade Mystery and Suspense

Rasputin's Scorn

Tears in the Water Playlist

1. "Summertime Sadness" by Lana Del Rey

2. "Where Is My Mind?" by Pixies

3. "Possum Kingdom" by Toadies*

4. "Midnight Special" by Creedence Clearwater Revival

5. "Sex and Candy" Marcy's Playground

6. "The Freshman" The Verve

7. "No Rain" Blind Melon

8. "Polly" Nirvana

9. "Today" Smashing Pumpkins

10. "Under the Bridge" Red Hot Chili Peppers

11. "Two Princes" Spin Doctors

CHAPTER 1

S he knew she was dreaming.

She stood at the end of the dock, looking at her reflection in the soupy water. Chestnut hair hung forward, framing a pale, oval face. She focused on her eyes, wide with fear, but also longing to see whatever was just beyond her vision.

The water rippled, shivering her image as she stood shaking. The air was warm, but her body ran cold, a result of her overwhelming anxiety.

She knew she was dreaming, but she couldn't look away.

There was something she needed to do, but she'd have to step into the water to do it. She couldn't go into the water—not after what had happened. She could never go into the water again.

An object was rising to the surface, dark and foreboding. She tried to tell herself it was a log, but wood didn't float after it had landed at the bottom of the lake.

She knew she was dreaming, but she waited.

She saw the white eyes blink and the mouth open, revealing a pink tongue that flitted out as if the creature was using it to smell her.

The being revealed its true form, but not its nature, as it broke free of the water and reached out to her.

"Ren, come join me."

CHAPTER 2

R en woke up bathed in so much sweat that someone could have thought she had fallen into the lake.

She patted the other side of the bed, a common practice for her since Kai's death. She kept thinking that she'd feel him there, signaling that the last few months were just a terrible dream, instead of the one she'd just experienced.

The birds chirped merrily from their perches outside her window, and Ren took it as her cue to begin her day. She skipped her morning shower, debating on a brisk walk through her enormous subdivision, and started a pot of coffee. The brew that had saved her from many sleepy mornings perked up her senses and blurred the edges around her dream.

The door opened, and Gonzo rushed into her kitchen, falling dramatically into a chair. He spread his long arms out in front of him and pressed his face to the seasonal placemats her mother had insisted on buying her.

"Coffee. Now."

Ren chuckled. "Well, with that kind of entrance, I will get his Highness some coffee."

Gonzo waved his hand, playing into her banter. "Cream and sugar."

She filled his cup and put in the additives. By the time she delivered it to him, Gonzo was sitting up.

"You're up early," she remarked.

"I had a client," he explained. "The guy couldn't wait until a reasonable hour to stop by the studio. He had to schedule a session at six o'clock this morning."

"It was a short session." Ren glanced up at the clock. "It's barely seven. I thought you needed more time—"

"He barely gave me enough time to get out my oils!" Gonzo interrupted. "He said he had to get to work."

"Couldn't he have set an appointment for after work?"

Gonzo rolled his eyes. "He said he had to get to bed *early*." He mimicked the last word in a voice Ren was certain didn't belong to the patron.

"Why didn't you go back to bed?"

Gonzo shrugged. "I saw your light on, and it looked like the perfect opportunity for me to share my woes with the privileged."

It was Ren's turn to roll her eyes. "I never would have been able to afford this place if it hadn't been for—"

She was going to say Kai, but she found it hard to speak his name. Giving voice to it made her circumstance real, and she wanted to avoid the subject of her husband's death as much as possible.

Gonzo sensed the shift in the mood, and he sought to correct it. "I know. We starving artists couldn't afford our digs if it wasn't for our wealthy benefactors."

He put a hand on Ren's arm, but the touch was brief. Gonzo had lost his parents just before he'd met Ren, and he covered his grief with wine and poorly timed humor.

A picture of his mother and father hung in Gonzo's foyer. He had inherited his name and pointed chin from his father and his small nose, pale skin, and brown eyes from his mother.

"So, I guess you're up for the day," he said.

"I was thinking about going for a walk. Do you want to come with me?" She stared at him over her coffee cup as she took a sip.

"You're just as offensive as my patron," he returned, smiling. "You early risers have something wrong with your brain."

"I'm a night owl, too," Ren interjected.

Gonzo didn't comment. They both knew her strange sleep cycle had started after Kai's death.

He lifted his mug in a mock cheer. "Enjoy your walk. Keep your app on in case you run into trouble."

Ren had installed an emergency application on her phone at her mother's request. She knew little about it, but she thought it would help the people she had added to her contact list find her if she were kidnapped.

Gonzo drained his mug and jumped up from the table, saluting her. "I'm off to bed. I'll see you again when normal people should be up walking around."

Ren laughed. "I think you have it a little backward, but I hope you sleep well."

"Plan to," he said before he left as quickly as he'd arrived.

She marveled at the ease of their exchange. It was hard for her to interact in social settings, but Gonzo made her feel comfortable—even when he pushed her boundaries.

They had only been close for about a year, but they had shared more than most friends who had known each other since their youth. Gonzo had been there for Ren during the most tragic times in her life, and most of the time, he let her pretend her demons didn't exist.

Ren threw on a pair of black leggings and a pink shirt that advertised the need for more funding to fight breast cancer. She wore it or a sunset orange shirt when she walked to make herself more visible to her neighbors. She tied her long hair into a high ponytail and set out, carrying her phone in one hand and her keys in the other. One key stuck out from the fist she made around it so it would allow her to throw a more effective punch if she were attacked.

Erwin was a quiet town in Northeast Tennessee. Other than the raging river that rolled through it, the town kept Ren safe from oceans and lakes. Occasionally, the creeks would rise, and she'd have an uncomfortable moment as she drove over a bridge, but for the most part, she was far away from the water above five feet in depth, just under her height.

Ren wound down the curling streets, throwing a hand up at faceless neighbors as they drove by. She'd never really gotten to know any of her neighbors, even though Kai had thrown a party when she'd moved into his house, inviting everyone within a five-mile radius.

Ren was a more solitary creature, preferring a good book and music to a rowdy night out with friends. Kai had enjoyed social gatherings, but he had compromised his desire for interaction with other people to sit at home with her and guess the identity of the killer on the thrillers they had watched.

An unexpected tear slipped from her eye, and she wiped it away quickly. She picked up her pace, and she was back at her door in minutes, panting, but feeling better than when she had set out.

Ren loved to exercise, but she wasn't interested in building muscle tone. When she was young, she'd had a group of friends who were obsessed over their weights. Even though they were all thin teenagers, they stood on a scale once a week to see who had lost the most weight. Whoever won got to eat a cream-filled doughnut as the others watched. After several weeks of watching her friends devour the delicious pastry in front of her, Ren set out to win, hiding her food, or vomiting it into jars when her mother grew suspicious. It wasn't long before Ren was gobbling the celebratory doughnut every week.

Her preoccupation with her size continued into her college years, but it changed when she met Kai. Just after they'd started an intimate relationship, he'd confronted her. Ren had tried to cover her skeletal form with baggy clothes, but Kai hadn't been fooled. He encouraged her to seek counseling, and Ren had gone willingly. She still saw a therapist, but her monthly appointments had turned into sessions where she vented about a guy who cut her off in traffic or waited too long for a latte instead of any real issues.

In the past two months, the problem had returned, and Ren counted every calorie and pushed herself through rigorous cardiovascular exercises. She knew she needed to discuss it with her therapist, but she felt too disconnected from the woman to bring it up.

The door beeped as she walked inside, and she hurried to push in the code on the alarm. Kai had insisted on extra security last year, and even though they lived in a nice town, they had a beautiful house with expensive things, so it seemed like a logical way to help prevent theft.

Her phone buzzed in her hand, and Ren lifted it. The call came across as a local number, and she answered it. Usually, she would have let the call go to her voice mail, but she had a feeling she wanted to hear first-hand the caller's reason for reaching her.

"Is this Ren Martin?"

"It is," she replied hesitantly.

"This is Alicia Young, from the realty company. I need to talk to you about the lake house."

Ren almost dropped her phone as she struggled to remain calm. She didn't want to talk about the lake house. In fact, she hoped it burned to the ground.

It was the last place her husband had been seen alive.

CHAPTER 3

"What are you going to do with it?" Gonzo asked as he chomped through a microwaved calzone.

Ignoring the bits of sauce that had dotted her table when her friend had spoken, Ren answered, "Do you have any matches?"

He sighed. "Really, Rennie. Are you gonna sell it?"

Ren had considered selling the property, but it would mean going back to the lake house. Something was there no one else could see, and she'd have to retrieve it before a nosy buyer started looking at every corner of the house.

"I thought about it, but everything is still too fresh."

Gonzo sat his half-finished calzone on the paper plate he'd brought over and reached for her hand. He grabbed her fingers, tugging lightly at them.

"I know this is hard," he said. "You have to make a few decisions. It's been almost a year since—" he was going to say Kai's name, but he rephrased his plea "—the accident. There are maintenance costs that come with a property of that size. You have a little money, but you don't want to throw it away and lose *this* house."

Gonzo had a point, and she'd thought about it. Kai had left her a considerable amount of money, but the lake house and their residential home weren't paid off, and they had several other outstanding debts. Kai had hired a caretaker for the lakeside property when he'd gained it, and the fee for his service was deducted every month. It was twice the sum Ren thought they should pay him, but Kai insisted the guy was good at his job. Ren thought the fee arrangement had a little more to do with Kai's years in school with the man who cared for the property, so she never mentioned her feelings about the bill.

"I'll think about it this week," she promised. "Selling the house would mean I had to go there, and I don't want to do that right now."

"You don't have to go back there," Gonzo cut in quickly. "You could let the realtor handle the sale and hire movers to take the stuff to storage until you're ready to sort through it."

Ren closed her eyes, attempting to think of the best way to relate her feelings to her friend. She opened them, and he was staring at her with his head cocked to the side.

"I had to do the same thing with Mommy and Daddy's beach house in South Carolina." he went on. "I loved it there, but I had to sell it."

Ren patted his hand. "It's not that. I'm ready to let go of the house, but I have something there I need to do." Gonzo still didn't seem to understand, so she added, "It's very personal to me."

Assuming it had something to do with her late husband, Gonzo let the matter drop. He finished his snack and brushed his fingers off over the plate. Ren took the empty plate to the trash for him. Gonzo's laziness would have annoyed most people, but Ren was glad to be doing something for another person.

Her back was turned to him when Gonzo asked, "Have you thought about dating again?"

The question threw her completely off guard, but her reply came quickly. "I'm not ready."

"Girl, I hope you get ready soon. Look at the guys on here."

When Ren turned around, Gonzo was flipping through his phone. Smiling men with varying features slid across his phone until he found one that interested him.

He held his phone up to her. "Like this one."

Ren gave the screen an obligatory glance, noticing blue eyes and dimples. "He's cute, but he's not my type."

Gonzo tsked. "He's hot, and that's *my* type." He got up, too lost in his phone to notice the chair he'd left pushed out. "Well, I think I've found my entertainment for the evening."

"I hope you have a great time with his dimples," Ren said, an involuntary smile spreading across her face.

"Oh, I plan to," Gonzo returned. "I have something that will fill them in."

"Gross, Gonzo."

Before he reached the door, he looked back at her more seriously. "If you decide to go to the house, I can go with you. I don't want you to have to do it alone."

Ren expressed her appreciation and watched him through the window as he crossed her backyard. When he pulled the latch on the fence that connected their yards, she moved into the living room, satisfied that Gonzo was safe on his property.

It was nice of her friend to offer to go with her to the lake house, but Ren had no intention of taking him up on it. If she went back, it would be alone. No one could see what she had to do.

CHAPTER 4

R en sifted through the mail. Most of the letters were bills that would be automatically deducted from her account. Ren needed to convert to electronic statements, but every time she sat down at the computer, it reminded her of the work she hadn't done.

Ren had been a writer for the past five years. Kai had encouraged her hobby into a profession, and Ren had three nonfiction works published. She'd been contracted to write another book, but she was nearing the deadline with a half-finished manuscript.

The book focused on the myths and legends that circulated about the town in which she lived. When she'd started her research, fueled by the mysteries she was trying to uncover, her world seemed perfect. It had been easy to interview the elders in her small town and look at the books written by authors who had died before she was born.

Ren had made many new connections during that time in her life. She'd cherished her conversations with the wise people in her community, and she called to check on them occasionally. She'd enlisted the help of a local psychiatrist who had explained the way the human brain seeks to develop reasons for certain unexplained occurrences in nature and answered her questions about mass hypnosis in the cases where people were rumored to have seen a strange event at the same time. Ren was glad she'd recorded her conversations with the doctor, as tragedy had struck before she'd had the chance to add his thoughts to her book.

Ren had gotten a little work done, but her output had diminished from five thousand words a day to as low as five hundred. The house reminded her of Kai, and it was hard to concentrate. She'd catch her eyes wondering to a photograph of their fifth wedding anniversary framed above her desk, or the bronze quill he had gotten for her after her third book had been published.

Ren had taken down the picture and put the quill on her night-stand, but her thoughts still drifted. Finally, she moved the items back into their proper places, as she enjoyed being around things that reminded her of that time in her life.

At the bottom of the mail stack was a letter from the fire depart-ment, asking when she'd like to schedule a time to fill her in-ground pool. She glanced through the window at the backyard.

The pool had been covered for two years. At her insistence, Kai had allowed it to be drained, but he was convinced that they'd refill it the following year.

Ren thought back to his encouraging comments.

"You love the water," he had said. "It won't be long before you're swimming like a fish again."

Ren hadn't wanted to disappoint Kai, as he enjoyed the water, too, but every time she thought about dipping her body into it, she went rigid with fear. Her experience, coupled with Kai's untimely death, solidified her need to stay away from the water.

"I don't care if the neighborhood kids turn it into a skate park," she voiced, ripping the letter from the fire department up and throwing it into the trash.

"Talking to yourself is the first sign of mental illness."

Ren's hand went to her chest before she saw the owner of the voice. "Gonzo! You scared me."

"I have that effect on a lot of people." He chuckled.

Ren tossed the rest of her mail on the counter. "I thought I locked my back door."

He pulled out a chair and plopped into it, resting his elbows on the table. "I can neither confirm nor deny the possibility of a locked door."

Ren put her hand on her hip, opened her mouth, closed it, and threw her hand into the air. "You know what? I'm not surprised. With everything else about you, it doesn't shock me you know how to pick a lock."

"Aww. Stop. You're makin' me blush." He covered his eyes in mock embarrassment.

She picked up a nearby dish towel and threw it at him. It hit his arm, and he rubbed the spot, even though he hadn't been injured.

"You brute," he admonished.

"You shouldn't just walk into another person's house if the door is locked. I could have been—"

"With a man?" he interjected.

Ren felt the heat rise from her neck to her face. "I was going to say *in the shower.*"

"Why couldn't you have been with a man?"

"I-I'm n-not ready," she stuttered.

"Well, I-I think it's t-time," he returned, imitating her.

Ren sighed. "I don't know if being your friend is good for me." She was only half-joking.

Gonzo sat back in his seat and folded his arms over his chest. "I don't know what you're talking about. I'm a peach of a person." He put his nose in the air when Ren snorted. "You're the one who isn't good for me."

Ren's eyebrows went up. "Really, Gonzo? How so?"

He turned around in his chair to fully face her. "First of all, you are overwhelmingly negative. Sometimes, I think the only word you know is *no*."

She shook her head but stopped when she realized she was making Gonzo's point for him.

"Secondly, you're hanging onto the memory of a dead person, and depression is a muse to some artists, but it's not good for me." He returned to a position facing the table. "I'm known for my vibrant colors."

Even though Ren was annoyed by Gonzo's assessment of her, she couldn't disagree with it. She was depressed, and it hadn't only affected her friend's creativity.

"I haven't been able to write." The admission was out of her mouth before she could stop it, but she didn't regret telling her friend.

"I know."

She stared at him quizzically. "How do you know?"

He put his head in his hands and rubbed his eyes. "You used to show me sections of your manuscript, but you haven't done it" —he paused to find the right words— "in a while."

Gonzo wasn't afraid to make Ren deal with certain truths, but he was still careful with her feelings. He had cared for Kai, too, and it had been hard for him to say goodbye.

"I don't know what to do," Ren confessed. "Everything in the house reminds me of him."

"You can come over and write at my house," Gonzo offered.

He had been kidding, but Ren knew he'd allow her to stay there indefinitely if she needed companionship. He had become her best friend, and she wasn't even sure how it had happened.

He faced her again, cocking his head to the side as he tried to read her emotions. "You should go somewhere."

That jolted Ren. "Where? Do you think I'd be any better on a beach somewhere surrounded by people?"

He brought his hand to his chin and ran his thumb and forefinger down his pointed beard. "Mabe not, but you have other options."

Ren's eyes widened as she realized his meaning. "Oh, no. That place would be worse than here. It has all his family memories from his childhood summers."

"I think it's time to finish whatever it is you feel you haven't done to get over Kai," Gonzo said, uttering his name for the first time in a year.

Ren opened her mouth to argue, but a reply didn't materialize. Gonzo was right.

CHAPTER 5

She stared at her packed suitcases. She always forgot something, no matter how many times she checked her list.

Gonzo had talked her into staying at the lake house for a week to write and set things in order before she sold it. She went over it in her head, but Ren couldn't remember how he had talked her into it.

She checked over the house one more time, adjusting the temperature and making sure the lights were off before she set the alarm and carried her suitcases to the car. The trunk of her mid-sized vehicle was spacious, and her suitcases didn't fill it, making her second-guess the items she'd chosen.

"I'm only going for a week," she said to herself, before shutting the trunk.

Ren had thrown a few bags of food in the backseat, along with a cooler. She wasn't certain how long it would take to have groceries delivered to the lake house, so she had taken some provisions.

Gonzo had been happy to liberate the rest of the perishables from her refrigerator, and he'd carried them off when he'd visited the previous night. To him, five o'clock in the morning was what most people considered just after midnight, so her friend wasn't there to see her off.

The drive was over an hour, but Ren entertained herself with good music. When she started to ascend the mountain, her satellite radio came in clearly, only blanking out in two spots as she passed rocky areas.

Ren guided the car around a curve, and the lake came into view. The sun had just peeked over the mountain, and it sparkled on the water, almost making it shimmer.

Ren felt bile rise into her throat, but she pushed it down, reciting a phrase her therapist had given her. "I am on land. I am okay." She must have been speaking it for the rest of her drive because she was still repeating the words when she pulled into the drive.

For a moment, the water was out of her view. She was enveloped in budding trees and evergreens until the driveway opened up on her property.

It was hard for Ren to think of the lake house as her own. Kai's parents had bought it when their son was young, but they hadn't enjoyed it for long after they retired. Kai had inherited the house and the surrounding land, complete with a pier to dock his boat. Everything Kai owned had transferred to Ren after he'd died, and even though the house on the lake was hers, Ren felt like an imposter, as she had contributed nothing to its purchase.

Ren stopped the car under a wooden carport at the back of the house. The house seemed menacing, but the water beyond it was more ominous.

She shook her head. It was just a house, nothing more.

The house was two stories high, with a basement underneath that was large enough to include a one-car garage. A wide porch wrapped around the bottom level, and a balcony extended from the upstairs master bedroom. Ferns hung from the porch at intervals, and the small yard and landscaping were well-maintained.

On the back porch, the grill had been uncovered. She wondered if the caretaker had used it, or if it was a detail he had overlooked after Kai's last visit.

A small boat rose and fell with the motion of the lake. Teenagers drove a pontoon boat too close to the shore, and the boat rocked with the force of its speed.

Ren grabbed the cooler and dragged it to the door. She entered the house through the backdoor, as the front of the house faced the lake. She smelled the crispness of pine outside and inside. Candle warmers stood sentinel in the foyer, dispensing the constant fragrance.

She carried the rest of her food and suitcases before she put away her provisions. The oak cabinets welcomed the addition of her snacks and soups, and the refrigerator still seemed bare when she added her condiments, salad, and yogurt.

"Maybe I do need to eat more," she commented as she stared at the space.

"What are you doing here?"

The voice startled her, and she jumped, throwing the door to the refrigerator wide in her distress. She stared at the intruder, unable to utter a sound.

He crossed the space between them, closing the refrigerator door. "You must be Kai's wife."

Her mind raced through the stranger's possible identities, and she arrived at a logical solution. "You're the caretaker."

His mouth formed a grim line. "I'm Jonas Kane. Your husband and I went to school together." He extended his hand, and Ren shook it.

"I'm Ren Martin."

"I know," he replied swiftly, withdrawing his hand and sticking it into the pocket of his light-colored carpenter pants. "I saw you here a couple of times with Kai before the accident."

Now that Ren knew the identity of the man who had followed her into the house, she noticed more about him, like his perfectly aligned teeth and straight nose. His prominent cupid's bow sat atop a thin lower lip and dimpled chin. Jonas was taller than her, but his baggy pants made him appear smaller than his full height. He had dark hair, like Kai's, but his eyes were a spring green with starbursts around the irises.

"Are you there?" he asked, drawing his coal-black eyebrows together.

"Yeah," Ren answered, embarrassed that she hadn't been paying attention to him as he spoke.

"I asked how long you'll be staying."

Jonas was the caretaker, so his question was a logical one. It had caught her off guard, and she strained her brain to remember a proper answer.

"I'll only be here a week."

Jonas visibly relaxed. "That's good. If you need anything, I'll leave my number on the refrigerator."

He pointed to a pad of paper and a pen that hung by a magnet before he busied himself with writing. Ren imagined Kia or his father had purchased the notepad, as they were the cooks in the family, and the pad had once been used for shopping lists.

Jonas was gone as abruptly as he'd arrived, and it was only after he'd left that Ren remembered her manners. "I should have asked him to have a cup of coffee."

She looked around, and she was relieved to see a coffeemaker on the counter. She made enough for a couple of cups and pulled a mug down and washed it. It was a cup that her husband had purchased during one of his trips to California, and the Golden Gate Bridge stretched across the front.

Ren walked through the house as she drank her first cup of coffee. The kitchen emptied into a cozy living room with a brick fireplace that had been painted white to help easily match the decor. Light blues and yellows still seemed out of place against the wooden walls, but Kai's mother had insisted everything look cheery.

The dining room boasted a long cherry dining table with eight chairs and a matching cabinet with shelves of glass, encased over three long drawers. The lake was in full view of the picture window, so Ren moved out of the room, past a half bath that had been added to a space that had once been an extended pantry, and climbed the wooden steps.

Thick stripes of non-slip tape ran along the edges to allow her to gain better footing as she climbed.

The upstairs was simple. A full bath sat between two guest rooms, and the main bedroom stretched across the front of the house. Except for the primary bathroom, the bedroom took up the front of the house.

Ren had no idea how she was going to talk herself into staying in that room. Its clear view of the water was almost debilitating.

She reasoned she could stay in one of the guest bedrooms, but they were small. She needed to stay in a space that afforded her the ability to move around, as her creativity would be blocked if she were in a small space.

"Gonzo said you needed to push your boundaries," she reminded herself.

She drained the last of her cup and walked downstairs for a refill. Along the way, pictures of her husband and his parents smiled happily at her. She couldn't help thinking that they didn't know about the horribly different ways they'd die when the photographs were taken.

"That's too morbid, Ren," she said to herself.

Still, in the center of the living room, as she stared at a family picture in which she was included, Ren wondered how she would die. *Would water prove to be the villain that stole her life, or would she slip away in her sleep at a bitter old age?*

Her preoccupation with death unnerved her, and she resolved to work on her manuscript. She pulled out her laptop, which was never far away, and watched the cursor blink.

She was between sections. She had just finished up the story about the terrible event that had haunted Erwin since 1916: the elephant hanging. She wanted to move into more current tales, but she was unsure whether she should start with the mother and daughter haunting of the Devil's Looking Glass or the claim that an Erwin sheriff who had died in the sixties had helped capture a serial killer last year.

Ren had written a paragraph leading into her decision when she heard a gentle tapping. The sun was shining through all the windows, but the air was still. It was a silence she could almost hear, so when the tapping stopped and resumed again, Ren knew she wasn't imagining it.

She moved from her place on the couch and followed the noise to its source. Her feet stopped at the half bath. She stared into the windowless room. The bright floral patterns made it seem innocuous, but something was making the sound.

Ren searched the room, but aside from a couple of hand towels and old medicine bottles, nothing seemed to be inside it. At one point, the sound rose to a maddening level, and as abruptly as it had begun, it silenced.

Ren was circling the bathroom when someone rapped on the door. She checked her hair and makeup in the mirror, and seeing that she looked tired and reasonably presentable, she made her way to answer it.

A bubbly blonde bounced up at her from the other side, holding a covered plate of what smelled like chocolate chip cookies. She pushed the plate into Ren's hand and moved past her, looking around at the high ceilings and dated decor.

"I'm Becky," she said, putting her hands on her hips and offering a too-wide smile. "Are you the new owner?"

Ren shook her head. "I'm Ren. This was my husband's vacation home."

Becky's hand flew to her mouth. "Oh! You poor dear." She put her hand on Ren's arm. "I thought, after what had happened, you'd sell this place."

Until that moment, everyone had taken it easy on Ren. They hadn't mentioned Kai's accident so openly. It took a moment to recover.

"I'm here to get it ready to sell," she said.

"Oh," Becky replied, drawing out the vowel. "Couldn't you have hired a realtor to do it? I mean, I couldn't imagine staying at the same place where—"

"I'm going to get it ready," Ren said, cutting her off.

Becky's face fell, but it pulled back up quickly. This time, her features were more genuine. "I'm sorry. I don't know what got into me. I mean, why is it my business what you decide to do with the house?"

Ren was still angry, but after Becky's apology, she invited her to have a cup of coffee. Becky accepted, and the two women talked for most of the morning.

Becky had gone to school with Kai, too, but she remembered little about him. She and her husband lived several houses down, and Ren had passed her property on the way to the lake house. When Becky saw the unfamiliar vehicle, she called the head of the neighborhood watch, and he told her that someone was staying on Kai's property.

"Let me guess," Ren said. "Jonas is the head of the neighborhood watch."

Becky pressed her finger to her nose. "You got it."

Ren tried hard to like the woman, but she couldn't get past the nagging idea that Becky was only there for gossip. She made the excuse that she worked from home, but Becky didn't seem to get the hint, staying another uncomfortable half hour. Becky had Ren plug her number into her phone before she left, but Ren doubted that she'd use it.

The house was blissfully quiet when Becky left, but no matter how hard Ren strained her ear, the tapping didn't resume. Ren went through the rest of her day with no more unannounced visitors or strange sounds. It was only when she turned the lights out that she got the feeling that she was being watched.

CHAPTER 6

"**I**'m in love!"

"You're not in love," Ren said. "Lust is not love."

"Well, I'm in love with his butt then."

"Still lust," she countered.

The line was silent for a moment, and Ren took the opportunity to move the phone from one ear to the other. It was much easier to scrub the bathtub while she balanced the phone on her shoulder.

"He's coming over again tonight," Gonzo went on. "I wish you could meet him."

"I'll be back in a week. I can meet him then."

"But what if he's gone?"

Gonzo's infatuations were as fleeting as the wind, so it was a distinct possibility. He'd had more lovers in a month than she's had in her life.

"Then I'll meet the next one," she joked.

Gonzo switched gears. "Have you seen anyone on that spooky lake?"

The way he phrased his question caused Ren to pause. "Why do you say it's *spooky*?"

"It's not really *spooky*," Gonzo backpedaled. "Well, maybe it is." He took a deep breath and let it all out with his words. "I knew a girl in college who disappeared after she took a trip to that lake with her friends. After that, every time I went up there, I felt like she was still there."

"I guess that is a little spooky," Ren admitted.

The line was quiet until Ren decided to answer Gonzo's previous question. "I've only seen the caretaker and a neighbor who brought over some cookies."

"Was he cute?" Gonzo asked, choosing to focus on the man.

"Who? The caretaker? I guess he was attractive." Ren could almost see Gonzo roll his eyes.

"Invite him over," Gonzo suggested. "Invite him to your room. Make passionate love until the dawn's early light."

Ren sighed heavily, but she smiled at her friend's insistence. "Probably not tonight."

"Why not? It's not like you're doing anything else."

Ren laughed at her friend's presumption. "I might be very busy with my manuscript, or there are a few things in the house I need to do before I call the realtor."

"Well, make sure he's one of the things you do before you leave," Gonzo insisted. "You won't ever have to see him again. It's perfect."

"Unlike you, I've had a little more substance in my relationships."

"All three of them," he mocked, huffing at her need for emotional attachment in sexual relationships.

It was true that Ren had only experienced three men in her life, but she was hurt that Gonzo had thrown it up at her. Most of their friendship had been full of happy banter, but she had related her sexual history to him in confidence, and part of her felt like that was breached when he used it to make a jab at her.

"I'm not interested in sex right now," she said, her voice a little colder than she'd intended.

"Well, I am," he returned, oblivious to her tone. "I'm going to get ready to have the time of my life tonight."

When she clicked off the call, Ren felt a little emptier. She wanted to work on her manuscript, but she decided to power clean the rest of the bathroom. She stood back and admired her work, satisfied with the look, but disappointed with the smell. At home, the scent of bleach permeated the air after she cleaned, but at the lake house, there was an undertone of something else.

Ren had gone to a Floridian amusement park when she was a child, and she'd smelled a swampy scent in the air and water. She assumed it was the same possibility at the lake house, but instead of a swamp, she was smelling the undertones of limestone.

She hopped down the steps to add an air freshener for the bathroom to her online cart, and she remembered leaving her phone upstairs. When she returned to the bathroom, she found her phone on the rim of the basin.

As she stood typing, something besides the clicking on her phone got her attention. At first, it was a gentle tap, but as Ren tuned her ears to the sound it became louder.

Ren had found the source of the mysterious tapping. *It was the pipes!*

It made her feel better to know the source of the noise, but her revelation brought about a new set of worries. "Who's going to fix it?"

She sighed heavily, realizing what she had to do. It seemed Gonzo was going to get part of his wish after all. She'd have to call Jonas over to assess the damage.

She left him alone after she'd shown him the source of the noise. "I heard it in the bathroom downstairs, too," she told him before she walked to the kitchen.

Jonas went to the basement, but he only stayed for a few minutes before returning to the upstairs bathroom. Ren watched him out of the corner of her eye, hating that she wanted him to show her more attention.

A bottle of red wine sat on the counter. She thought about opening it, but she was afraid her loneliness paired with Jonas's good looks and Gonzo's suggestion would be too much with the alcohol.

Instead, she pulled a soda out of the refrigerator and returned upstairs to offer Jonas one. He accepted it, wiping his forehead with the back of his hand.

"It's already pretty hot this year," he commented.

"The weather is always a little strange in the spring. Then we have blueberry and blackberry winters in May."

That's only sometimes," he interrupted. "The water is almost warm enough for diving."

"You dive?' Ren asked.

"Sometimes," he answered, putting his tools back into his toolbox. "Do you?"

Ren felt the nervousness in the tops of her thighs, and she leaned against the door frame for support. "I used to."

He turned around and responded with concern. "Are you okay?"

She smiled and tried to stand a little straighter. "Yes. I just can't talk about the water without thinking about Kai." She hadn't said his name a lot since his death, so the note it left in the room almost echoed against the wall. Perhaps it was only that her husband's name resonated so deeply with her.

"I'm sorry," Jonas said, rising from his spot on the floor. "I wasn't thinking."

He put a hand on her arm, and Ren had to will herself not to jump at his touch. She'd grown accustomed to Gonzo's brief hugs, but she wasn't used to someone else touching her, especially someone she didn't know.

"It's okay," she responded automatically. "It happened almost a year ago, but it still feels fresh in my mind."

"I get it," he responded, rubbing his thumb over the place he touched on her arm. "I miss him, too."

Ren hadn't stopped to consider how close Kai and Jonas had been. They had known each other since their early middle school years when Jonas had moved to Tennessee from another state. Aside from that, she knew very little about her husband's friend.

"You knew him longer than me," she conceded. "I'm sorry for your loss, too."

Ren hadn't expected his eye to glaze with tears. He blinked them away before they fell.

"Would you like a glass of wine?"

Her invitation was sudden, and she hadn't meant to speak it. She thought she may have made the offer out of an obligation to make him feel better.

"I have to go," he said, his voice husky from his unshed tears. "Maybe some other time."

"Of course," she said, feeling the sting of rejection, even though she'd only meant to be friendly. "Thank you for checking on the pipes."

"It shouldn't be an issue," he said, turning to pick up his toolbox. "The foundation was laid about a century ago, so there are going to be creaks and groans. I tightened up some things, so you should be good to go."

Ren walked him to the door, and she was ready to shut it when he spoke.

"Call me if you need anything else." He gave her a soft smile that Ren thought was a little sad, and he walked out into the night.

She watched him cut through a break in the trees that lined the property, and she remembered that Kai had said that his friend lived next door to the lake house.

Ren went to sleep that night thinking about Jonas's green eyes. She woke up the next morning to someone standing over her.

CHAPTER 7

"What are you doing here, Gonzo?"

He plopped on the edge of the bed, and the pressure from his thin body caused Ren to roll uncomfortably. She pulled herself up and rested against the headboard.

"I was at a party," he slurred. "Some people weren't very nice."

Ren panicked. "You didn't drive, did you? You know I would have come to get—"

He held up his hand and then looked at it with amusement. Ren closed her eyes and sighed when she realized a little more than alcohol was responsible for her inebriated friend.

"I called a service," he said, holding up his phone. It slipped from his hand and tumbled to the floor. Gonzo looked at it, but he made no move to bend over to retrieve his phone. It was probably best, as Ren didn't think he could steady himself enough for the action.

"I thought you were going to be with your guy with a cute butt?"

"I was," Gonzo confirmed. "It was his friend's party."

Gonzo's eyelids drooped, and his blinking slowed. He moved his feet across the rug to gain purchase, and Ren groaned inwardly when she realized he hadn't taken off his shoes, and he was raking mud across the light blue rug.

"What happened?" Ren asked.

Gonzo shook his head and looked out the window where the sun wouldn't crest the mountain for another hour.

"They don't think men should date each other."

Ren put her hand on his arm. "Did everyone at the party feel that way?"

"No," he admitted. "There were other couples there, but for some reason, this big, bald guy, who was wearing a flannel shirt that hadn't been washed since Elizabeth Taylor was a child, thought he should tell me his opinion about it. So I punched him."

Ren felt her breath escape her. She would never have expected that reaction from her friend. "You did what?"

Gonzo gave her a half smile. "He was out cold." He raised his fists to mimic the action, but he pulled himself too far forward and had to sway to correct himself. "My dad taught me how to box."

"What about the guy you were with? Didn't he offer to help you get home?"

"He may have paid for my ride," Gonzo said, trying to access a memory that escaped him. "I think he was going to go with me, but—"

Ren waited for Gonzo to finish his sentence, but he never did. Instead, he struggled out of his shoes.

When he lay on the pillow beside her, Ren wrapped her arm around him. Soft snores echoed in her room, and Ren found it hard to go back to sleep. She pretended the warm body against her belonged to her husband when their relationship was new, and she was able to drift into a peaceful doze.

It was their anniversary, and they had gone to a nice restaurant in a nearby city. The Bohemian art made her feel more comfortable, but it clashed with the dress code and menu.

"We can go somewhere else," Kai offered. "I read it had great reviews."

"It's fine," Ren told him.

She tried to pick something off the menu, but she was unfamiliar with elevated French cuisine. She allowed her husband to choose her meal and hoped he knew her sensitivities well enough not to order an item she couldn't eat.

The server approached their table, and once it was established that both he and Kai spoke French fluently, their conversation morphed into a battle of who could talk with a better accent. Ren thought the server sounded more at ease as he spoke, but she smiled encouragingly at her husband.

When the food was delivered, Kai asked, "None of the food has cinnamon?"

The food runner confirmed the chef had been informed of Ren's allergy and had taken great care with their selections. Ren was glad the men conversed in English, so she could understand them and didn't have to interrupt their pleasant conversation with a question about it.

"You look beautiful," Kai told her.

The young woman at the next table looked up and smiled at her. The attention caused Ren to blush. It was true that she'd gone to great lengths to look especially lovely, but she was uncomfortable with the attention.

"You sparkle like the stars in the sky," Kai went on.

Before she could stop him, Kai was on his knees in front of her. The surrounding people turned in their seats, expecting a couple on their way to the altar, but they didn't know Ren and Kai were already married.

He slipped a diamond ring on her left hand. It dwarfed the square diamond beneath it and drew every light in the room, reflecting each one in a different direction. Ren marveled at the size of it and felt her hand was heavier with the weight.

"Will you marry me?" Kai asked. When Ren's eyebrows rose, he whispered, "Again?"

Ren squeaked out her answer, and Kai announced, "She said 'yes'!"

The room erupted in applause. Ren wanted to hide under their table, but she forced herself to wave at the people who were congratulating them.

"We're already married," Ren commented after their desserts were delivered.

"I love you so much that I want to marry you again," he said, grabbing her hands. "And you seemed conflicted between wedding dresses, cakes, and a theme, so maybe another wedding will give you a chance to enjoy a less stressful ceremony."

It was a sweet gesture, but Ren didn't know how a forest full of their family and friends would be any different from a beach with their wedding guests. Any gathering made her anxious, but she didn't want to ruin her husband's happiness with her insecurities. He wanted to make her happy, and Ren was going to play the part.

"It sounds lovely," she said.

"Now, except for the dress and any lingerie," he said with a wink, "tell me what you're planning."

He'd offered the option to her less than five minutes beforehand, and Ren hadn't made any plans. She drew on her alternate choices from the first time she had planned their wedding.

"I think we should renew our vows at the border of the Cherokee Forest, and—"

He cut her off, waving over the server and ordering their best champagne. "I'm sorry, Lauren. Tell me more."

Kai was the only one who called her Lauren. Ren was an uncommon name, and she believed Kai was trying to set himself apart from her other lovers by referring to her by what he thought was her full name. She could have corrected him, but the first time he'd made the mistake was during an act of love, and she hadn't wanted to sully the experience. She told her family and friends not to say anything to him about it when they mentioned his mistake to her, and they complied.

"Will it be near the Nolichucky River?" he prompted.

She nodded, taking a drink of her champagne. The bubbles seemed to travel from her nose to her head, and it wasn't long before the people in the room faded into the background.

"I know how much you love the water," she said. "If you want, we could get married at the lake house."

His blue eyes clouded over, and he put his glass on the table. "No. I think it's better to get married near the Nolichucky River."

Feeling chastised, Ren stopped speaking. It took Kai several tries, but he finally encouraged her to talk again. He could always coax her out of her shell.

They shared their hopes for the wedding until the bottle of champagne was gone. Ren didn't object when Kai ordered another bottle, but she was unsure about his ability to drive when he tripped out of the restaurant.

It was one of Ren's biggest regrets. For if she'd spoken up, or taken charge and ordered a ride, then they would have made it home that night.

CHAPTER 8

Gonzo didn't wake until almost four in the afternoon. Even after he stumbled to the kitchen table, it took two cups of coffee and five blueberry waffles before he was acclimated.

Ren sat at the table with a novel she was only half reading and waited for her friend to open up like he had the previous night. Gonzo wasn't as forthcoming with his feelings, and it was different to see him so contemplative.

"I have to get my car," he announced.

Ren closed her book, not bothering to mark her page. "I'll take you."

They rode in silence. Ren attributed it to Gonzo's uncertainty. He may have been wondering if his car would still be there when they arrived, and if it was, in what condition they'd find it. However, Ren thought his mind was circling around his boyfriend.

Ren was a little nervous when she pulled into the driveway. For all she knew, the man who had verbally assaulted Gonzo could still be there, and a person with wounded pride was capable of many unsavory things.

Ren hadn't met the man upon whom Gonzo had bestowed his affections, but she saw her friend's face light up when he came out of the door of the house. He opened Gonzo's door and hugged him.

"There's my little heavyweight champion," he told him, staring at Gonzo with admiration.

Gonzo blushed, but he said, "I'd be a lightweight."

The men laughed and shared a kiss. Gonzo pushed his hands through the man's bottle-blond hair as he almost laid himself over Gonzo. The man was almost twice Gonzo's size, but given her friend's thin physique, the guy only had an average frame. Ren was feeling uncomfortable when Gonzo broke the contact and motioned to her. "This is my friend Rennie."

"Ren," she corrected, offering her hand.

"I'm Blane," he returned. "Is that short for Lauren?"

Hearing the name her husband had called her almost made Ren lose her breath. She still hadn't processed her dream from the previous night, and she was curious about the reason she'd had it while lying in bed with Gonzo.

"No," she answered. "I was named after a water flower."

"Oh, yeah," Blane said. He had a long nose, but his dimples and perfectly straight teeth offset it. "Gonzo said you used to take underwater pictures."

Gonzo stared sharply at Blane, and Blane closed his mouth with a snap. It was true Ren was still sensitive when others discussed the water, but she didn't want Blane to get the wrong impression about her.

"I haven't done that for a couple of years," she told him. "I write novels now."

Blane was happy to be thrown a conversational lifeline. "Have I read anything you've written?"

His smile was contagious, and Ren found herself at ease with him. She could see Gonzo's attraction to Blane and the reason he had stayed with him longer than his usual fling.

"I doubt it," she said. "I write nonfiction books, and most people find it boring."

"I like nonfiction," he said.

"She doesn't write about serial killers," Gonzo commented and turned to Ren. "Those are literally the only books in his bookcase."

"I beg your pardon, sir," Blane interrupted. "I'll have you know I possess the fine works of Lewis Carol."

"A well-known pedophile."

As the men argued playfully, Ren thought back to the feelings she'd had at the beginning of her relationship with Kai. Just as the two of them had been perfect for each other, she believed Gonzo and Blane were, too. Their arguments were more like banter, and smiles danced across their lips as they spoke about subjects other people might find offensive.

After their discussion died down, Blane put his hand on Gonzo's arm. "I was worried about you. After you punched Dan, it was chaos. I looked everywhere, but I couldn't find you. Why didn't you answer my texts?"

"I was drunk," Gonzo said. "I'm lucky I was able to get my driver to Ren's house. I didn't know the address, but he seemed to know the house when I described it to him."

Kai had thrown a party at the lake house several years ago, and Gonzo had been invited. One of his boyfriends had driven him, so

Gonzo hadn't noticed more than a little of the passing scenery and the house.

"Who was he?" Blane asked.

Ren heard a note of jealousy in his question, but it wasn't overwhelming. To her surprise, Gonzo answered him kindly.

"Don't worry, Blanie. The man was married and totally uninteresting."

It struck Ren it was the first time she'd heard Gonzo say his lover's name. He had used the same ending he had attached to her name, too, indicating that he did it for everyone close to him. When she thought back to his references to his parents as "mommy" and "daddy," it made more sense to her. She was proud of her psychological assessment until their conversation took an uncomfortable turn.

"I looked through the whole house for you," Blane went on. "And then I went outside and checked the shore. I was scared you'd fallen in and drowned."

Blane was close to tears, but that didn't keep Gonzo from issuing a sharp jab to his ribs. Blane was annoyed by the contact, but his eyes widened when he realized he'd ventured into a taboo area again.

"You don't have to watch your words around me," Ren offered. "I'm in therapy, and my husband's been gone for almost a year."

Blane didn't seem convinced, but he kept talking. "It's just that I had read about a girl they found dead, and the one that was with her hasn't been found."

"Here?" Ren asked, at a higher octave than she'd intended. "At this lake?"

Blane nodded solemnly. "They were college students who wandered away from their group."

Gonzo sighed. "They were two girls who wanted to find a private area to experiment with each other. They were too drunk and ended up drowning."

"I don't think so," Blane said.

Gonzo crossed his arms. "Then why aren't the police treating it as murder? They're just looking for the other body."

"It's a serial killer," Blane insisted.

"Because two girls died," Gonzo said. "I highly doubt it."

"It's not just the two girls."

That time, Blane received a jab that rocked him backward. He issued a cough and rubbed the place where Gonzo had injured him.

"What's going on?" Ren asked. She bounced her eyes from Blane to Gonzo, but neither man would look at her.

"It's nothing, Rennie," Gonzo finally said. He kissed her cheek and hopped out of the car, almost entangling himself with his boyfriend, before Blane moved. "Thanks for the bed, food, and free therapy session." He counted off each thing she'd provided for him on his fingers as he listed them. "I'll call you tomorrow."

"If I let you up for air," Blane joked, patting Gonzo's butt.

Ren drove back to the lake house. She blared music from her radio so she wouldn't feel alone in the empty car. She tried to sing along to the music, but her thoughts kept going back to the girl who had drowned or was presumed dead.

Had they really drowned in the water due to their intoxicated state, or had they been drowned? The latter seemed unlikely, as one of them had been found, and the police weren't calling it a murder. She debated looking up the story online, and when she got back, she pulled out her computer and located the news article about the incident.

A photograph of both girls popped onto the screen. One was blonde, with a high forehead and a broad nose, and the other one was brunette. The brunette wore dark red lipstick and had crystal blue eyes. They were both nineteen.

The article repeated the same story she'd heard from Blane. Seeing no other information, Ren closed her laptop.

She snapped to attention when a knock sounded at the door. She approached it cautiously, only opening it when she'd established the identity of the person on the other side.

Jonas held up a bottle of wine. "I thought I'd take you up on your offer, but I brought my own bottle."

CHAPTER 9

"I hope you don't mind," he said.

Ren opened the door wider, letting in a breeze that had been churning springtime smells. "Not at all. Come in."

Jonas looked around as if he were searching for someone. "I'm not interrupting anything, am I?"

"No," Ren answered, drawing out the vowel.

"I saw a man get into your car with you this morning, and I—"

Ren saved him the trouble of finishing his sentence. "Oh! That's just my friend, Gonzo."

Jonas raised a dark eyebrow.

"He'd be more into you than me," Ren explained.

That seemed to clear it up for Jonas. He grinned sideways and set the wine on the counter. He knew just where to find the bottle opener, but that was no surprise to her, as he cared for the house, and he'd been there when Kai had thrown parties. Ren didn't remember seeing him a lot during the festivities, but she was busy trying not to feel overwhelmed by the number of people who wanted her attention. She was thankful for the guests who could entertain themselves.

Ren was a little disappointed Jonas had selected a white wine. She usually drank red, convincing herself that her indulgence was simultaneously improving her health. When he offered a toast, she tipped her glass to his and swallowed almost half the glass.

The toast had been to their new friendship, but Jonas seemed guarded. There was a darker side to the man in front of her than there had been on the day he had startled her.

"I guess you'll be leaving this weekend," he remarked.

Ren took another drink of her wine and realized she'd almost finished the glass. She slowed down and took smaller sips. Unfortunately, she wasn't used to white wine —or drinking it so fast— so it seemed to go straight to her head.

"I might have to stay a little longer," she answered. "I have to get the place ready in case I want to sell it."

She hadn't wanted to tell Jonas, but the wine had loosened her tongue. She'd been afraid that he would be upset with her, as part of his livelihood depended on the money he received from caring for the lake house.

His mouth formed a grim line, and he took a sip of the wine. Then his face straightened. "I understand. I'm sure it's hard for you to be someplace where Kai had so many memories."

His words struck her, but she wasn't certain why they provoked any response from her. It was an innocuous statement. After all, her husband had lived in the lake house, and he'd vacationed there many times as an adult.

"I'll be sad to see it go," Jonas went on, "but that's what happens."

"I'm not having the place torn down," Ren said, suddenly upset. It was unlike her to speak out, and it surprised her. "I'm sorry. I must have had too much wine."

Jonas picked up the bottle and tipped it toward himself. "To be honest, I don't drink wine. I bought it as a friendly gesture since you offered some to me the last time I was here. The clerk at the store seemed to think it was a good one, but it's made me feel a little sick."

Ren was glad that she wasn't the only one who had suffered from the alcohol. "Maybe we should stick to coffee and cookies next time."

He nodded, and a genuine smile lifted his features. One of his eye teeth was slightly crooked, and it humanized him. She felt more comfortable talking to someone who had noticeable flaws while hers were buried beneath her polished appearance.

"I'll let you pick the coffee since I failed miserably with the wine."

They laughed, but after the rings of their shared joke had echoed off the walls, nothing followed it. Ren hoped Jonas would leave, and he seemed uncomfortable enough to suggest it, but he stayed. Maybe he thought there should be a certain length of time attached to his visit.

"This is really hard, isn't it?" he said.

Ren was shocked. She was thankful he'd addressed their obvious awkwardness, but she was surprised he'd admitted his feelings about it openly.

"Yes," she agreed, but she was afraid to say more. She didn't know if she would hurt his feelings or upset him.

"It's my fault." He ran a hand through his hair. "I've never been good at meeting people. Kai used to introduce me to kids at school, and they considered me a friend, but only because I hung out with him." He looked at his hands before his eyes found her face. "That's why this is so hard for me. I don't really know how to talk to people, and then you invited me to drink with you, but you're also Kai's wife."

He was rambling, so Ren saved him from further embarrassment. Normally, she would have put a hand on his arm to comfort him, but in light of his previous statement, she thought he might have conflicting feelings about her, so she spoke over him.

"Jonas."

He snapped out of his diatribe and focused on her.

"I'm pretty introverted, too. Kai forced me into a lot of uncomfortable situations, like parties and dinners, but it made me a better person."

"None of the people he introduced me to have contacted me since I came up here to stay," Jonas said. "Do any of his friends call you?"

Ren had to admit she'd been alone since Kai's funeral. A few of his friends' wives and coworkers had checked on her for two weeks after the interment, but after a month, Ren's only contact had been Gonzo.

"No."

"Looks like we're in the same boat," he said, draining his glass of wine, even though he'd mentioned it had made him feel ill.

Jonas got up and pushed in his chair, holding the sides of it as he leaned over the table. "I think I've spread enough joy this evening. I'll go home now."

Ren didn't know whether she should feel anger or pity for Jonas as he made his way out. He had been in a horrible mood, but he seemed genuinely upset about involving Ren in his troubles as he slumped out.

Ren's eyes threatened to close as she sat at the kitchen table. She decided to go to bed early, as the wine coupled with her sleeplessness after Gonzo's arrival the previous night had depleted her energy. She had trouble climbing the steps, but once she was in bed, she passed into her dreams quickly, and thankfully, she didn't remember any of them.

Chapter 10

"**Y**ou're staying longer." It wasn't a question.

"Yeah. It should only take another week." Ren folded a red sweater, but she thought better of it and put it back into the drawer. Instead, she added a light blue tee shirt.

"Are you sure it's a good idea?" Gonzo said, pacing through her bedroom as she added more clothes to her suitcase.

She shrugged. "Nothing's happened since I've been there."

"Have you gotten any writing done?"

Ren paused before she resumed packing, her green halter top in her hands. She felt like she'd been caught, but what exactly had her friend unearthed? Was she just embarrassed that she hadn't been able to produce more than a couple of pages of usable manuscript since she'd arrived at the lake house? Still, it was more than she had written since Kai had died.

Gonzo nodded to her green top. "That one looks good on you. I wonder if he'll like it."

Ren colored. "Who?" The word had popped out automatically and Gonzo narrowed his eyes.

"Well, you're going to be out in the middle of nowhere, wearing a halter top I last saw you in when you went dancing in the city, so there must be someone there you want to see you in it." He tapped his chin. "It must be the caretaker!" He feigned excitement and immediately dropped his features.

Ren had thought Gonzo had wanted her to gain the attention of the opposite sex. "It's not like that," she said. "We had a cup of coffee, and it was awkward—"

He nodded along with her explanation. "It's awkward because he's weird."

"He's not weird," Ren defended, but she wasn't sure. She dropped her top on the folded clothes in her suitcase and sat next to her friend on the bed. "What's wrong with him?"

"Mainly, he's boring. There's barely a mention of him online."

"When did you research my caretaker?" Ren asked.

"Ages ago," he answered, but when Ren didn't ask a follow-up question, he added, "When you said you were going up there alone."

"Why did you do that?" Ren asked.

Gonzo laughed. "I had to be sure you'd be safe. You're not really observant when it comes to people."

"Yes, I am," Ren argued, but she couldn't find an example fast enough.

Gonzo shook his head. "You wave at Pete Rosen every morning."

Ren gave him a questioning look. "Who's that?"

Gonzo let out a deep breath. "Pete Rosen lives two blocks up in a blue house. He has that ugly red truck sitting in his front yard."

Ren remembered he was a tall man with a flat face. "He's a nice guy. We wave at each other every morning."

"I know," Gonzo sighed. "I checked him out after you dragged me along on one of your morning torture sessions."

"Walks," she corrected.

"Whatever. Anyway, he's on the sex offender list."

Ren's eyes widened. "Why is he out of jail?"

He patted her shoulder. "You're so naïve. People rarely serve life sentences for rape." He patted her back. "That's why I say you're a little under-observant. Pete Rosen stares at you like you're his next meal."

Ren groaned. She recalled when Gonzo had asked her to walk at the track or in the mall before it opened. She had laughed at him, but now she understood his concern.

"Why didn't you just tell me?"

Gonzo stood up and picked up her top, folded it, and added it to the growing pile in her suitcase. "There are times to tell you things, and there are times when I let you find out on your own. Pete Rosen wasn't an immediate threat. I would have found a way to wind him into our conversation, but this Jonas guy..." He met her eyes. "Something's not right about him or his brother."

"He has a brother?" Ren asked.

Instead of answering her, Gonzo took her hands and pulled her to her feet. "You won't listen to me if I tell you not to go back, but will you be careful?"

Ren nodded. They hugged, and she zipped up her suitcase, promising to call Gonzo every day she was gone.

Before she left, she went to her drawer and slipped something into the side compartment of her bag. She doubted that she'd use it, but it was good to be prepared.

Ren stuffed the bikini in the back of a drawer. She was glad she had put it into her bag before she'd left, but she didn't know what had given her the idea to do it. She couldn't even look at the water, let alone swim in it.

Gonzo had mentioned Jonas's brother, and Ren was determined to find out about him. After an hour's search revealed nothing about the pair, she made dinner.

It was simple and depressing to make a meal for one person. She could have anything she wanted, but she couldn't share it with anyone.

Before the accident, Kai had cooked for her almost every day. He seemed to enjoy his time in the kitchen, singing the Italian songs he played as he chopped and diced the vegetables.

Necessity fueled Ren's experience, and the only thing that made her happy was reading after the food was ready. Books couldn't provide conversation at the table, but they gave her a way to escape her current circumstances, and that was enough for her.

She decided on meatless spaghetti but changed her mind before she cooked the pasta. She cut a fourth of an Italian loaf and cooked the marinara sauce while the bread got crispy in the oven. It was a short, but satisfying, meal.

When she finished washing the dishes, she heard the sound. This time it was clearly coming from the kitchen sink, and it was louder than it had been when she'd heard it in the bathrooms.

She debated looking into the problem herself and decided that she wouldn't know what was wrong if she found it. She dialed Jonas's number and told him about the issue. He was in a better mood than he had been when they'd shared the wine, and he agreed to come over right away.

Ren brushed her teeth and hair and straightened the house in the time it took him to walk to her door. He smiled at her openly, but he went straight to work on the problem, as Ren stood uncomfortably at the kitchen counter with her arms crossed over herself.

"I may have to order a new part," he commented, more to himself than to her.

"I'll pay for whatever you need," Ren volunteered and wished she could suck back in the words. He was making the repairs to her property. Of course she'd be fronting the cost!

He smiled at her, and Ren felt an uncomfortable feeling in her stomach. It was such a contrast to the way she'd felt about him when he'd shared the glass of wine with her.

"I'll take care of everything, and I'll send you a bill."

He glanced around the room as if he were assessing it. "Do you still plan to sell the place?"

After speaking with Gonzo, Ren was more confident about her decision. "Yes."

Jonas hung his head. "I guess change is inevitable. I'd invite you out on the water to see the true beauty of this place, but you're too scared to go."

Ren's first reaction was offense, but her temper cooled quickly when he didn't follow it up with another comment. She searched for a way to defend herself from his previous comment but only arrived at a weak statement.

"My husband took me out on the lake."

"I'm sure he did," came Jonas's curt reply. "But he didn't take you to the place I'm talking about. If he would have shown it to you, you never would have wanted to leave."

Ren was getting increasingly flustered. Someone who simply heard Jonas's words wouldn't think they were meant to upset her, but if they examined his tone and partially clenched jaw, they'd realize that he was attempting to incite her anger.

He had mentioned her fear of the water and insinuated her husband didn't value her enough to take her to the part of the lake that was most special to the people who lived around it. It was enough to drive her mad!

She searched for something witty to say, but as always, the words escaped her as she was in a heated moment. She stood at the door with her arms crossed.

Jonas looked back at her once before he saluted her and left. She thought she heard him chuckle before he hummed a tune about sitting on a dock on the West Coast.

She closed the door deliberately, congratulating herself for not slamming it. She paced back and forth for several minutes before she'd gathered herself enough to prepare for bed. She had just touched the banister on the stairwell when a light knock stopped her.

Upon identifying the caller, Ren opened the door, but she didn't let him inside. Jonas seemed fine with standing on the porch, and he didn't move forward to push the issue.

His mouth turned down in the corners, and he put his hands in his pockets. Ren wondered if he was ever going to speak and tried to think of something to fill the awkward space before he opened his mouth.

"I'm sorry." He met her eyes. "I was really rude to you."

Ren noticed his hair was brushed back instead of parted on the side. The look suited him, but it was probably the effect of running his hands through his hair as opposed to combing it before he'd left his house.

Ren had practice with men and their apologies. She didn't forgive him right away, opting to hear the speech she was certain he'd recited before he'd knocked on her door.

"I was friends with Kai for a long time, and when he died, it hurt me. I guess part of me blamed you for taking him away from here because—"

Jonas stopped, realizing he had hit upon multiple sore spots. As she watched him battle his emotions, Ren couldn't feel angry with Jonas. She felt the need to comfort him, even though his apology had been more damaging.

Ren touched his arm, and Jonas recoiled. The action surprised her, and she took a step back.

His eyes widened when he noticed he'd offended her. "I don't have many people touch me," he confided. "I'm usually only around my brother."

"I shouldn't have—" Ren started, but he stopped her.

"It's not your fault," he said. "You were trying to be nice."

They stood awkwardly with the wind blowing circles across their faces. There was a hint of pine in the air that flashed a memory too faint for Ren to grasp.

"I'd like to make it up to you," Jonas went on. "Can I take you on a picnic?"

Ren's initial reaction must have been clear, as Jonas backpedaled. "We can stay away from the water. There's a spot on the mountain" —he pointed to the north of where they stood— "and it..."

He trailed off, but Ren got the idea. "I think that would be nice."

A grin spread across his features, revealing the most genuine smile she'd seen from him. "Okay," he said, waiting a moment before he repeated himself.

They made plans for the following afternoon, and Ren watched him walk away. He took a path to the right of the one she had seen him take previously, and Ren wondered how many paths Jonas and Kai had cut through the woods over the years of their friendship.

Thinking of Kai brought pain to her heart, and she regretted making plans with his friend. It felt like she was cheating on Kai, even though he was dead. She debated canceling her date with Jonas and decided against it. A reasonable amount of time had passed since her husband had died, and Jonas had proposed nothing more than friendship.

She thought about what to wear the following day, and her mind wandered to the day she met Kai.

CHAPTER 11

"I'm sorry," he said.

Nothing was going to take the dripping coffee off her white blouse. She was glad it hadn't been intentional, but she didn't carry extra clothes with her.

"That's okay," she said after he'd run to the nearest food cart for napkins. She didn't mean it, but the man seemed so distraught she couldn't add to his distress.

He started wiping the stain, oblivious to its location, until she took his hand away from her breast. Upon realizing his mistake, the man's face colored.

The red danced across his features, complimenting his blue eyes and raven hair. She saved him from further embarrassment by introducing herself.

"I'm Ren. I thought you should know my name since we've gotten so close."

She'd hoped to make him laugh, but his face almost turned purple before he stuttered. "I-I'm, K-Kia."

Ren was terribly shy, and she avoided contact with most people, even when they surrounded her. She recognized his discomfort, and her heart went out to him.

"Hey, Kai. I'm glad to meet you. Do you work around here?"

Kai looked up at the brick building behind him as if he were just noticing it. "Uh, yeah. I'm a partner." He pointed to the sign that read: Martin and Martin.

"A lawyer," Ren observed. "You know what they say about lawyers, don't you?"

He seemed genuinely bewildered. "What's that?"

Ren was having fun as she kept the conversation flowing. "I don't know. I hoped you could tell me."

She had expected him to laugh good-naturedly and go on his way, but he asked, "Do you like sports cars?"

Ren understood an invitation was forthcoming, and she didn't want to interrupt its flow. "Yes."

He had gathered more courage as their conversation progressed, so Kai had no problem asking her to go for a ride with him after he left the office. She accepted his offer, and they spent an enjoyable evening together. Kai was as smooth-talking with Ren as he was in the courtroom, and it wasn't long before she was waking up in his bed most mornings.

Once he got comfortable with their routine, things changed. He still bought her flowers and whisked her away for late-night dinners, but he was gone for most of the day, as his job required long hours of meetings and research.

Ren was used to spending time alone, so she relished his daily absences. They provided her with a way to recharge before she interacted with him again. Kai saw no difference in her behavior, as he was distracted by the demands of his work, until the first day he took off to spend time with her.

The morning had been beautiful, with delicious rays of sunshine dancing through every window. At first, Kai's suggestion to go out on the water seemed like a great idea, but after they'd had breakfast and packed up the car, Ren regretted her willingness to go on an excursion with him.

Kai talked about the people he knew, and he was excited about introducing her to his parents, but Ren's mind was full of dread. She wasn't ready to meet Kai's family, but she couldn't tell him.

He had just passed the county line when he asked her if she wanted to hear another song on the radio.

"I don't care," she responded hastily. "Whatever you want."

"Hey," he responded, taking a new tone and easing up on the accelerator. "What's wrong?"

"I'm just tired."

Kai wouldn't let it go. He had been around her long enough to know that something was wrong. Finally, she told him about her shyness.

To her surprise, he pulled over. He gave her his full attention, turning off the car and moving in his seat until he faced her.

"Have you talked to anyone?" he asked.

He meant a psychiatrist. Ren hung her head.

"Good," he said, surprising her. "I want you to talk to someone I know. He has good methods of—" Kai stopped himself and held out his hand. "I'm sorry. I'm always doing that. Do you *want* to talk to someone about it?"

Ren took his hand, but she didn't look up. "Yeah. I probably should."

He squeezed her hand and pulled on it to let her know to look up at him. When she did, she noticed a sincerity she hadn't fully expected. Kai had always been kind to her, but it seemed she was seeing his genuine nature for the first time. At that moment, all their barriers were down.

"I'm falling in love with you," he confessed.

They didn't go to the lake that day, and they stayed on the side of the road for a long time before they changed directions. On their way back to Kai's house, they stopped for a meal.

The food was good, and when Kai went to the register to pay for it, Ren took the opportunity to visit the ladies' room. Sobbing echoed from the stall beside her, and Ren tried to ignore it. She fixed her hair, as it was still disheveled from her experience with Kai in the front seat of his car. She was smiling to herself about it when a woman burst through the door.

There was nothing remarkable about the woman, except for her vibrant purple hair. She walked briskly to the closed stall door and addressed the person behind it.

"Sweetheart, we have to go."

"They have to find her," sobbed the voice.

The woman's eyes darted to Ren, but Ren pretended not to see her. "We can talk about this at home."

"But where's Delaney?" the voice asked. "Why can't they find her?"

Ren saw sandaled feet under the door. The shape of the legs and the young voice led her to believe that the person in the stall was the woman's teenage daughter.

"The police are doing the best they can," the woman said. "But right now, I need you to get out of the bathroom, Augusta."

Ren left Augusta and her mother to talk about Delaney. She met Kai at the door, and they left.

Ren played with the radio, and Kai hummed a tune she didn't recognize. She settled on a song she didn't hate and watched the glittering water as she rode.

"I think there's a missing girl," she said.

Her words seemed to startle Kai, and he jerked to attention, causing the car to dip onto the shoulder before he corrected it. "Oh." He seemed to strain in his attempt to act casual.

"Yeah," Ren said, drawing out the word in her hesitation to continue. "I think her name is Delaney."

"Delaney Mathes?" he questioned.

"I don't know," she answered honestly. "There was a girl in the bathroom who said she was missing."

"That's terrible," Kai said. "That's really terrible."

"Did you know her?"

He rubbed his eyes with his forefinger and thumb. "I know her family. I know all the families that live around the lake."

"Do you think they'll find her?"

Ren wasn't sure why she asked Kai that question, but he seemed prepared for it. He looked at her out of the corner of his eye before his hands tightened around the steering wheel.

"They never do."

"What do you mean?" Ren felt like she was treading in deep water, but she was too curious to stop asking questions.

Kai's jaw clenched, but he released the pressure quickly. "It's probably a good thing we didn't go out on the water today."

Chapter 12

R en hadn't thought about Delaney's disappearance since the day she had talked to Kai about it. In the wee hours of the morning, it poked at her, causing her to rise much sooner than she'd anticipated.

She crept across the room and opened her laptop. It was never far from her side, even though she could seldom write.

She typed Delaney's first and last name into a search engine, and after weeding through several social media suggestions for women with the same name, she arrived at an article about the disappearance of a sixteen-year-old girl.

The online article stated that Delaney and her friend had been out on tubes on the lake. Her friend fell asleep, and when she woke up, Delaney was gone. Her tube was found deflated on a group of sharp rocks.

The authorities dragged that part of the lake, but they didn't find Delaney's body. A trail of blood was found in the woods, but it stopped after only a few feet. In an updated article, Ren learned the blood had been tested, and it was confirmed to match Delaney's blood type.

Ren unearthed everything that had been made public within two articles. She wasn't sure why she felt the need to search for Augusta, but she texted Jonas for their address without a second thought. Instead of an address, he messaged directions, and Ren took a shower before she drove to the house.

The house was a little grander than the one she had left, and its new paint reflected the late-morning sun. She had a passing thought about showing up unannounced, but as with any social interaction, if she didn't do it as soon as she thought about it, she'd find an excuse to stay home. There was something pressing in her mind about the missing girl, and a quick calculation between the disappearance and the one Gonzo had mentioned proved she wasn't the only one.

Ren almost lost her nerve after she knocked on the door, but the occupants of the house were nearby and one of them opened the door almost immediately. The girl stared at her with wide brown eyes.

"Do I know you?"

Ren guessed she had been the girl in the stall on the day she and Kai had stopped at the lakeside restaurant. She held out her hand in a friendly greeting, but the girl only stared at her.

When she'd met Kai, Ren had worked for the local newspaper. She used some of her skills from that time to soften the situation.

"I'm Ren Martin, and I'm following up on a story about Delaney Mathes."

The girl's face crumbled, and her knees gave out. Her mother was at her side almost immediately.

Her hair was blue instead of purple, and she'd lost a considerable amount of weight. The skin around her face sagged, giving her a much older look than her eyes and voice suggested.

"When will you people stop!" she yelled at Ren.

The woman's reaction startled Ren, and she took a step back. "I'm sorry. I'm not even with the newspaper anymore. I was only trying to find out what happened to Delaney."

"We wonder the same thing every day," the woman barked at her.

Ren hurried to her car after the woman produced a gun, and she sped off their property. Her legs were still shaking when she climbed her porch stairs, and she didn't calm down until late afternoon.

The sun started to set, and she knew it would get cooler, but Ren didn't reach for her jacket. She wanted her skin to absorb as much of the sun as possible before the heat was gone.

"Why did you want the Hernandez's address?" Jonas asked. "I didn't think you knew them."

"I don't," she admitted. "I woke up with a crazy notion, and instead of sorting it out, I bothered those poor people."

Jonas was understandably confused, so Ren told him about her experience in the restaurant's bathroom and her feelings about that disappearance and the other ones around the lake.

"People drown in the water all the time. It's not like it's happening every week."

Jonas realized his mistake when Ren's face paled.

"I didn't mean—" He scrubbed his face, rubbing the fashionable stubble on his cheeks. "I'm sorry. I wasn't thinking about what happened to—"

"That's okay," Ren said in an effort to keep him from finishing his sentence. She already felt bad enough for going on a picnic with one of Kai's friends, and the mention of her deceased husband's name would make the situation more awkward.

Jonas had been packing up the food they had shared, and he brought a bottle of red wine to the blanket spread out on the ground. He sat beside Ren, but at a distance suitable for two friends talking and enjoying a country sunset.

"Look," he said. "I've lived at the edge of the water for most of my life, and there are always disappearances. People get caught under the current, or they drink too much and pass out in the water. There are times when the best swimmers will hit their heads on a rock, and—"

He noticed Ren's growing unease and held his hands up.

"I'm only saying this because stuff like that happens, but it doesn't happen all the time. Thousands of people go out on this lake every year"—he motioned to the body of water just beyond their range of sight— "but only a handful of them have bad experiences. They've even found some of the missing people you're talking about."

"They didn't find Delaney," Ren said.

"Maybe not," he conceded, "but Roger Jones was found in a shed at the edge of the Fairmont property. He'd gotten confused while he was fishing and had wandered into the nearest shelter."

Ren raised her eyebrow. "Men go missing, too?"

He let out a forced chuckle. "Yeah. The water doesn't play favorites."

His dark words made her think about Kai again. She was introspective for a time, and Jonas was silent. In retrospect, he was probably trying to think of a way to change the subject, but Ren was so absorbed with her own worries that she wasn't aware of his internal struggle.

He lifted the bottle of wine. "I think you like red. That's right, isn't it?"

Jonas seemed so fragile. Ren doubted that he'd made many friends or been on a lot of dates, so he was genuinely concerned about her preferences.

She nodded. "That's actually my favorite."

Jonas uncorked the bottle. "It's like the one on your counter."

Ren laughed inwardly. Of course he had seen the bottle on her counter. Like her mother, Ren always kept a bottle there for decorative purposes. It may have seemed strange to some people, but there were always two bottles of wine in the house, the one on the counter and the one that was chilled in the refrigerator.

"You look beautiful tonight," he said. Then his eyes widened. "You look beautiful all the time, but..." He fumbled for the right words but couldn't find them.

Seeing him flustered put Ren at ease and amused her, even though she shouldn't have indulged in the latter. She put him out of his misery quickly.

"Thank you. I think you look good tonight, too. I like your shirt. It brings out your eyes."

"Thanks," he replied, looking down at his shirt. "It's my brother's."

"What does your brother do?" Ren asked, attempting to start a casual conversation that would lead them away from anything embarrassing.

"He hangs around the house," Jonas said. "When our parents died, they left us a lot of money, so we don't have to do anything."

"Oh." His answer had only formed more questions in her mind. "Why did you want to care for the lake house if you didn't need the money?"

His response was quick. "Kai insisted on it. He trusted me."

She must have had a skeptical look on her face, as he added, "He made me take the money. You can quit paying me if it makes it easier for you. I would prefer it if you didn't pay me anymore."

Ren's mouth worked up and down, but no sound came out. Jonas rested his hand on her arm.

"I like you, Ren, and it wouldn't be fair for me to take your money."

Ren was conflicted. Part of her wanted to insist that Jonas carry on their paid arrangement, but another part of her was caught up in his light green eyes and the dimple winking at the corner of his mouth. Jonas leaned toward her, and she froze in place until their lips touched.

Ren's body came alive, and she struggled against it. She was compelled to continue to honor her husband's memory, but she wanted to feel a man's touch. She sent Jonas mixed signals by kissing him and pulling away before kissing him again, and he finally made her stop. They were both breathless as they stared at each other. He said nothing, and Ren was uncertain whether either of them would speak.

A call from below them interrupted whatever would have happened between them. They both turned to the sound, only to find a wild goat perched on the hill.

"I think I should go back," Ren said.

Jonas didn't argue with her. After they picked up what was left of their picnic, she climbed into his old truck, and they rumbled back down the hill.

She climbed out without a backward glance and hopped up her steps. She didn't offer Jonas a kiss goodnight, but she thought he understood the reason for her hasty retreat. If she kissed him again, he would have been going into the house with her.

Jonas messaged her about another date, and she responded with a positive, open-ended statement. She wanted to see him again, but she had to sort out some of her feelings first.

Her emotions emptied another bottle of wine, and she was almost certain she called Gonzo at some point, but the night became an uncomfortable blur. She passed out on her couch downstairs with the bottle dangling from her fingers.

Sometime in the night, she woke to the sound of beating. It could have been someone at the door, but it sounded like it was coming from inside the house. Then she dreamed of Jonas and decided he was the one at the door. He covered her with a quilt spread across the back of the sofa and told her to go back to sleep, so she drifted back into a heavy doze.

When she woke the next morning, she didn't know if she had seen him or if she'd imagined him, but she was still under the quilt.

CHAPTER 13

Becky stared at her over her cup of coffee.

Ren shook her head. "I'm sorry. Did you say something?"

Becky sighed irritably. "I asked if you had decided whether you were going to live here or sell the place."

"Oh," Ren acknowledged. "I'm not sure yet. This place meant a lot to my late husband, but it's a drain on my resources."

"I can imagine. The taxes alone must put a significant hole in your budget." She tossed her shimmering hair. "I have a small, 2,500-square-foot house, and the taxes are three times what we pay for our house in the city."

Ren was in no mood to entertain her neighbor, but she didn't have a convenient excuse to send her away. She wouldn't have opened the door for her, but she had thought Becky was Jonas when she knocked.

"I have a lot of work to do today," she said. She sat back in her chair and stretched, hoping Becky would take the hint.

"Did Jonas keep you up late?" She winked at her.

Ren was flabbergasted. She didn't know anyone had discovered her date with Jonas.

Becky giggled. "Girl, all the lake folks talk. Janie Ruble saw the two of you on the hill behind her house. She said you guys were about to get *indecent* before her goat screamed at you." She put air quotes around the word *indecent*.

Color exploded across Ren's face as heat traveled up from her chest. She was horrified that someone had seen her make out with Jonas, and she was mortified that the person had shared it with everyone in the community.

Becky grinned. "Don't feel bad about it. If I wasn't married, I'd be all over that man."

"I wasn't— I didn't—"

Becky smiled so widely that Ren could almost see all her teeth. "You shouldn't be embarrassed. You're both single." She looked at a perfectly polished nail. "Well, I guess he's single after what happened with Colette."

She looked up at Ren and measured her reaction. Ren hadn't invested her feelings in a relationship with Jonas, so she was unconcerned with the tidbit of information Becky had purposely slipped.

Ren's lack of curiosity didn't seem to faze Becky. "Oh, you know how young girls are. They overreact and run off in the middle of the night."

"How young was she?" Ren asked, abandoning her effort to remain uninvolved in gossip.

"I think she was twenty-two or something," Becky answered. "She was mad that Jonas didn't go to her college graduation."

"He may not have been with her long enough—"

Becky tsked. "They were together for two years." She leaned forward, and her hair almost spilled into her coffee cup. "Jonas never goes down the mountain."

The news wasn't so strange to Ren. She hardly left her house, or wherever she was staying. She'd been a little more outgoing before the accident, but that seemed like a lifetime ago.

"I can't say a lot about—"

Becky didn't let her finish. "No one's ever seen him venture too far. I think his brother gets things when they can't have them delivered, but Jonas stays behind."

Ren was curious about Jonas's brother. Even though she didn't like to gossip, she found herself asking, "Have you seen Jonas's brother?"

"Plenty of times," Becky replied, taking a drink of her coffee with one hand and setting her cup at her elbow. "He's a" —she trailed off in search of a word that fit— "jerk."

Ren raised her eyebrows. She hoped for more information, but she decided not to ask.

"No one likes Riley, and he doesn't care. We don't see him a lot, though, and when we do, he's out on the lake with his loud boat."

Ren tried to look sympathetic. She hadn't heard an overly loud motor since she'd been staying at the lake.

"He gets out when he knows no one is patrolling the water, and he spins it around. He almost killed my husband once while Bob was sitting in his fishing boat."

Ren tried to appear shocked. The range of emotions she had to show to continue their conversation was taxing her. She'd need a nap after Becky left.

"The man is unruly, and if he keeps it up, he's going to end up hurting someone one day." She huffed and threw a blonde strand of hair back over her shoulder. "I doubt he'll even care. He didn't even cry when his parents died, and that's a sign of a psychopath."

Ren disagreed, but she didn't argue with Becky's assessment. She had sobbed hard after Kai's death, and she was numb at his funeral. Tears may have glided down her cheeks at the interment, but her weeping wasn't nearly enough for the common perception of a grieving widow.

Thankfully, Becky had a hair appointment that dragged her away from Ren's table. She asked Ren to go with her, but Ren faked a headache, and it was believable, as Ren was exhausted from her conversation with Becky.

After a brief nap, Ren made herself sit in front of her computer for an hour. Her efforts translated into two good paragraphs and more fatigue.

She was preparing dinner when a knock startled her. She thought it had come from the bathroom, but she heard nothing when she stood in the room quietly. The doorbell echoed through the house, and she hurried to answer it.

Jonas stood on the porch, and when he saw her, he wrapped her in his arms. Ren returned his kisses, but she didn't feel the urges she had felt during their date, so it was easy for her to pull away.

"What's wrong?" he asked. "Don't you like me anymore?"

"I do like you," Ren told him, even though she felt a little uneasy about his forwardness. "I'm in the middle of making dinner. Do you want to stay and eat with me?"

"I was hoping to get to know you a little better," he said, raising his eyebrows suggestively.

Ren's stomach flopped. The last time they'd been together, it had been hard for Ren to pull herself off him, but now that he was making the advances, she couldn't get away from him fast enough.

She didn't want to sleep with him, but she acknowledged she was sending Jonas mixed signals. She thought it might be best to talk to him about it.

"Can we sit down?"

He narrowed one of his eyes at her, but he followed her into the living room. Once she had distanced herself enough to talk to him, she told Jonas some of what she was feeling.

"I'm attracted to you, but it's weird to get close to you when you were friends with my deceased husband."

Jonas picked at his tooth before he responded. "That is weird."

His acknowledgment was only a statement, and he didn't add to it. It left Ren in charge of moving the conversation along, and she was surprised where she took it.

"I don't think it's right for me to see you. I'll be leaving soon, and I'm going to put the house on the market."

That seemed to get his attention. "You're still selling the place?"

His outrage was clear, and it almost frightened her. She softened her voice and prepared to lie.

"I don't know yet. I may just keep it."

He relaxed marginally, but there was an edge to his features. He no longer had a cocky half-smile.

"I'll tell you what," he said, standing. "Why don't you call me when you figure out what you really want?"

He gave her a rough kiss, and then she was alone.

The stillness crept over her, and she thought about what she was going to tell Gonzo when he asked if she'd had exploits. She'd wanted to sleep with Jonas during their date, and then she'd rejected him. Maybe his attitude was a buffer against his hurt feelings.

She decided to go to his house and sort it out. She was either going to sleep with Jonas or call him out for his apathetic reactions. Maybe both.

Chapter 14

Ren followed the trail to the house Jonas shared with his brother. The two-story structure had recently been upgraded with newer vinyl siding. The long windows stretched from the floor to the ceiling in some rooms, but they were slender, revealing only small shards of light. The additional rooms on the ground level yawned out so close to the lake that the back of the house seemed to float in the water. In reality, the house was a safe distance from the lake, but the late hour concealed the shore and rocks between the house and the water.

As she had flown down the path, Ren had argued with herself about going to Jonas's house. It wasn't like her to show up anywhere unannounced, but there was something about him that attracted her and simultaneously repulsed her.

Ren didn't like entitled men, but she had always been drawn to people who exuded self-confidence. She assumed she surrounded herself with people who displayed strong egos, as she was lacking in that area. Jonas may have been introverted, but he knew what he wanted, and it secretly thrilled her he wanted her.

She didn't know what she was going to say, but she imagined Jonas would take over the situation when he saw her on his porch. Gonzo had told her about some of his chance encounters, and she was eager to have her own to share with him. Ren had reigned in her desires throughout her life, opting for the safest options, and she'd only stepped out of her comfort zone a handful of times, so she was nervous and exhilarated.

Raised voices carried to her through the open windows. Two men were arguing, and they didn't show signs of stopping.

Her body temperature dropped a few degrees, and she was hyper-aware of her presence in front of the house. If one of the men opened the door, they'd find her shivering at the foot of their steps.

"What did you think you were doing?" one of them yelled. Ren was almost certain it was Jonas, and her suspicions were confirmed when the other man defended himself.

"I was just having some fun," he declared in a pitch that was only slightly higher than his brother's voice.

"What you call 'fun' is dangerous! Do you know what could have happened?"

Becky had told her about her husband's near brush with Riley out on the water. Ren assumed Jonas was berating his brother for it.

"But nothing happened," Riley spoke as if he were soothing a temperamental child. "You make things seem a lot worse than they are."

A twig snapped loudly, and Ren glanced over at a deer who had wandered into the yard. Because the noise was so loud, or the brothers had trained their ears to hear specific sounds, the argument stopped.

Ren took the opportunity to announce her presence, and she knocked on the door. She only waited a handful of seconds as muffled commands were issued and a set of hurried feet bolted up the stairs.

Jonas was surprised to see her, but he tried not to show it. Instead of inviting her inside, he stepped out onto the porch with her and closed the door tightly behind him. He ran a hand through his hair, brushing it back.

"Hey, Ren," he said, seeming unsure about the best way to handle her presence. "What brings you over here?"

All the courage she'd had before she'd heard the brothers fighting seeped out of her. She stood at the edge of the porch, wishing she'd taken the same initiative as the deer and run off at the first sign of being noticed. Given his reaction, Jonas wouldn't have guessed that she had been in his yard.

"I-I n-need to borrow a cup of sugar," she stuttered.

Jonas's posture relaxed. "Were you really coming over here for sugar?"

He wasn't as cocky as he had been when he'd visited her earlier, and it made Ren feel more comfortable. She decided to be honest.

"My friend thinks I need to move on," she said. "I like you, and I think I may have been rude when I pushed you away—"

As she'd explained her feelings, Jonas's eyes had grown wide. She caught a glimpse of the man who had tried to make her his conquest, but it was in the form of anger. The cloud of darkness left his features quickly, and Jonas blinked into a more compassionate expression. He guided her to the porch swing and took her hand when they sat down. She let him rock them, but the swaying motion didn't calm her frazzled nerves.

"I think we should talk," he said.

Ren had always considered the phrase redundant. The person should simply begin speaking, as saying it only incited anxiety in the other party.

"I think you're beautiful, and I like spending time with you, but I'm still getting over someone."

"But I thought—" she started, but the tears in his eyes made her stop speaking.

"She left me," he went on, as a tear slid down his nose and landed on his lap. He hung his head, intentionally avoiding Ren's stare.

"I'm sorry," Ren said.

His smile was sad, and the heavy sigh that escaped him spoke of the weight he carried with him. "If I don't think about it, I can almost pretend she was never here."

He glanced up at Ren and then looked away quickly. "She had dark hair and blue eyes, too."

He didn't have to say that reminded him of his lost love. Ren had already figured it out.

"She was probably too young for me, but I fell hard for her." He shrugged his shoulders. "I don't know why. We really didn't have a lot in common." He looked into the distant night sky. "Maybe I was just lonely."

Ren understood what he meant. She hadn't known she was floating lifelessly out to sea until Jonas's attention had been thrown her way like a life preserver.

"I didn't mean to pressure you," she said, squeezing his hand and releasing it. "I just thought—"

He held up a hand to stop her. "I've been sending you some mixed signals. Like I said, you're beautiful, we seem to like the same things, and you seem to be content away from people."

Ren wasn't shocked he'd picked up on her introversion, but she was a little embarrassed he'd mentioned it. She hopped off the swing and leaned against the porch railing.

He jumped up and crossed the distance between them, placing a hand on each of her arms. He searched for her eyes until she looked at him. She was unwilling to reveal her feelings, but his response was sincere.

"Can we go slow?" he asked.

Ren had expected him to tell her he wanted to be friends, so she was surprised at the turn in their conversation. She was almost grateful that she hadn't gone through with her original intention. She had only been in steady relationships, and a fling wasn't really for her.

"Okay," she agreed. She wanted to say something more, but her lips wouldn't move to form more than one word.

"Okay," he echoed with a smile that brought the dimple on the right side of his face to life. "Can I see you tomorrow?"

She agreed to another date, and Jonas insisted on walking her back down the trail. She was thankful to have him by her side as they traveled back down the short path. Without her nerves dogging her steps, Ren was free to notice the gnarly tree roots and hanging branches that dangled like arms ready to grab her. She was surprised she had navigated her way to Jonas's house without stumbling or running into a branch.

"I never really cleared it out," Jonas told her when he noticed she was looking at their surroundings. "I still used the trail when I checked on your house, but it grew up a little since there weren't three little boys running up and down it."

Ren opened her mouth to ask him about his brother, but he was staring at her with admiration. She didn't want to ruin the moment.

"I have a confession to make."

They had arrived at her porch steps, and Ren turned to him, giving him her full attention. The sounds of water rushing to their ears made it a little harder for her to concentrate, but she did her best to put it out of her mind.

"I've read your books."

Unlike most authors, who would have felt their souls had been exposed in the pages of their novels, Ren was merely amused. "You wanted to learn about the history and folklore of Northeast Tennessee."

He glanced away and scratched the back of his neck. "Not really. I was more interested in the woman who wrote them."

She thought about what she could say and decided words wouldn't express how she felt. She lifted on her toes, and he met her lips. Their kiss melted her into place, and Ren was lost in it, forgetting the sounds of the nearby lake and the darkness surrounding them.

She was happy. But if Ren had known what the next month held for her, she would have run away and left Jonas where he stood.

Chapter 15

"It's getting boring here," Gonzo whined. "You said you'd be gone another week, but you've been there forever."

"Three weeks is not forever."

"It is to me," he pouted.

Ren smiled and balanced the phone on her shoulder. "Isn't your special man holding your attention anymore?"

He let out a sigh. "Yeah, but he's on a trip. His company sent him to some stupid art conference."

A laugh escaped her lips. "You know you're an artist, right? I don't think I'd be calling his conference stupid."

Ren heard the shift in the sound as Gonzo walked outside. "It's only stupid because he couldn't bring me with him. So I'm stuck here while my boyfriend is off meeting interesting people and doing interesting things."

"He's your *boyfriend* now," Ren commented.

"We're not labeling it, but yeah."

"How does he introduce you to his friends?" Ren asked.

"As Gonzo the Magnificent, the best lay in the known universe—"

"Okay, okay," Ren said, squeezing her eyes shut to block out the images she was likely to see if he went on with his self-proclaimed titles.

Her friend's response told her what she wanted to know. His tone had remained the same as he spoke, slightly playful and light. Gonzo and Blane were in a relationship, but Gonzo was too scared to admit it. If he said they were together, and something happened between them, Gonzo would be hurt. Ren was familiar with the feeling.

Gonzo had bounced from one lover to the next, but Ren had assumed her friend would fall head over heels for the right man. Blane treated him like a king, and Ren was glad they were happy together.

"When is he coming back?" she said.

"In a thousand years," Gonzo replied dramatically.

Ren heard the door close behind him, and she imagined him flinging himself onto his sofa like a distraught movie vixen.

"Why don't you come up to the lake house for a few days?" she proposed.

He let out a melodramatic breath. "And watch you mope around and avoid the water that's practically at your back door? No, thanks."

"Really," she went on. "Just because I don't go out onto the lake, doesn't mean that you can't come up here and have fun."

He was silent for a moment as he considered her offer. "Will you try to go on a boat with me?"

"No."

"Will you sit on the shore while I go swimming?" he tried again.

"Not a chance."

"You drive a hard bargain, Mrs. Martin, but I accept."

With Gonzo there, the house came alive. It no longer seemed like the walls were pushing against her, and Ren enjoyed the freedom. Alone, she had let her anxieties mount, but Gonzo pushed her focus outward, keeping her thoughts in the present instead of creating past or future worries.

When he parked beside her car, Ren went out to greet him. Gonzo threw her a salute and ran past the house, onto the dock, and jumped into the lake. Ren yelled after him, but she wasn't afraid when his body hit the water. She knew he would resurface unharmed, and he did, his long breaststrokes showing strength in swimming he hadn't revealed to her.

Gonzo was weighed down by his dripping clothes, and he'd ruined the shoes that squished up the porch steps. Ren wasn't prepared when he hugged her, wiping his face on her shirt.

"I have towels," she said, trying to dance away.

He held her firmly as he shook his head, spraying droplets on her face. Ren closed her eyes until the motion stopped.

"I'll definitely need to change now," she giggled.

Satisfied he had made her at least half as wet as him, Gonzo stepped out of his sneakers. It took some effort, but they came off and thunked against the open door. He kicked them to the side and walked past her, staring at the outdated decorations.

"This is so depressing," he said. "Where are the purples? Didn't these people believe in the colors of nature?"

"There are blues and yellows in nature," Ren countered.

He rolled his eyes and picked up a couch pillow with an overused geometric pattern. "Can we say, 'I'm a bored housewife with nothing but my cream puffs to keep me company'?"

Ren swatted his arm playfully, and he dropped the pillow. "They're dead. Have some respect."

"I will respectfully redecorate," Gonzo said.

Ren followed him as he sloshed through the house. His socks made imprints on the wood flooring, and Ren knew she'd be the one to clean it up.

"Could I get your suitcase out of the car?" Ren asked, hoping he'd take the hint and change into dry clothes.

"No. I'll get it later."

Gonzo tried to open the basement door, pulling it with all the force he could muster. "It's stuck."

Ren tried the door, too, but she couldn't get it to budge. "That's weird. Jonas was able to open it easily when—"

Gonzo didn't let her finish. "So you *have* been banging the hot caretaker."

Ren had known she'd have to tell her friend about her new interest, but she'd thought she could lead the conversation into it more naturally. She wasn't prepared for her cheeks to color, and for Gonzo to point at her with a self-satisfied smile.

"I knew you had it in you, Rennie." He guided her to the couch.

Ren was a little concerned about the watermarks he was sure to leave on the cushions, but she tried to put it out of her mind as she told him about Jonas. "There's really nothing to tell. He wants to take it slow."

"No man in his right mind will be able to take it slow around you," Gonzo affirmed. "When will you see him again?"

"He's supposed to pick me up at eight."

Gonzo waved her up. "That's not a lot of time. We have to get your hair and nails done, and—"

He stopped speaking when Ren stayed in place. She crossed her arms over her chest, her shirt still damp from Gonzo's hug.

"I'm not going anywhere," she affirmed. "My hair is fine, and I can do my own nails."

He bounced back onto the couch, his weight hardly moving her. "Fine. Home makeover it is. But I'm going to need your full cooperation."

Realizing that she was out of excuses, Ren submitted to Gonzo's pulling and fluffing until he made her into what he thought was a better version of herself. And as she looked in the mirror, she was glad she had let him do it.

Gonzo opened the door when Jonas arrived. Jonas kept throwing curious glances at Ren, for even though it was clear Gonzo wasn't attracted to Ren, he still seemed to want clarity on his presence.

"Hey, buddy," Gonzo said, adopting a drawl he thought matched Jonas's speech. "Where're ya takin' my girl?"

Ren gently pushed Gonzo to the side, offering an apology to Jonas. Gonzo's clothes were mostly dry from his impromptu swim, and Ren hoped he'd shower and change while she was gone.

"I can't take him anywhere," she remarked.

"I didn't know anyone was staying here with you," he said.

"I'll just be here for a few days," Gonzo piped up. "And don't worry. If the date goes well, I have some noise-canceling headphones." He threw them an exaggerated wink.

"It's time for us to go," Ren said as she rushed Jonas out the door.

Gonzo stood on the porch and waved as they climbed into the vehicle. "You kids have fun, ya hear!"

Ren buried her head in her hand. "I don't know what gets into him sometimes."

Jonas chuckled. "It sounds like he's a good friend." His eyes widened as Gonzo smacked himself on the butt and jumped in a circle like he was riding a bucking bronco. "With a questionable sense of humor," he added.

"Do you like living here?" Ren asked.

Jonas looked out over the cliff and stared at the lake as he answered. "I wouldn't live anywhere else." He breathed in the pine scent floating in the breeze. "It's peaceful."

"I love the view from here," Ren said, pointing to the sun setting on the horizon. "Thank you for bringing me."

"It's one of my thinking places. I come here when I can't be around my brother."

Ren was an only child, but she'd wanted a sibling. She had always felt like something was missing from her life and a sibling would have given her the special connection she needed.

Now that Jonas had mentioned his brother, she thought it would be a good time to ask about him. "How long do you think you'll live with your brother?"

"Until I move in with you," he said, but Ren caught the mischievous twinkle in his eye. "No, really. I don't know. I guess we'll live together until we kill each other."

Ren shifted her feet, and Jonas laughed. "We don't really get along, but we love each other. He's just infuriating."

"One of the neighbors said he was a little reckless."

Jonas's eyes flashed. "Which one?"

Ren moved a step away. "J-just one of the people around the lake. You know how gossip—"

His features softened, and he stepped closer to Ren. She allowed it, but she looked around for people who might help her if his temper flared. There was a couple fifty feet away, but they were too caught up in the landscape to notice them unless she screamed.

"I'm sorry if I scared you," he said. "I'm protective over Riley."

Ren relaxed, realizing that she didn't understand the dynamics between siblings. Apparently, they could hate each other, but one wouldn't let anyone talk about the other.

"It was Becky," he guessed.

When Ren said nothing, he nodded. "I thought so. She's a busy-body. Riley doesn't like her." He laughed without mirth. "But it didn't keep him from sleeping with her."

"But she's married!" Ren shouted before she could stop herself.

Jonas shrugged. "He's slept with all the women around the lake, except you."

"Is that why you didn't want me to see him last night?"

Jonas seemed to consider it. "Yeah, that was definitely part of it. He has a way with women. I'll never understand it." He put his hands in his pockets and rubbed the tip of his boot through the dirt. "He doesn't treat them well, but the meaner he is to them, the more they seem to want him."

Ren looked for a way to steer the conversation away from Jonas's brother. "Do you have any hobbies?"

"You wouldn't believe me if I told you."

"Try me."

He looked away and watched the last of the sun disappear behind the mountain. "I like to scuba dive."

The ground felt like it slipped out from under Ren. "Oh," was all she could manage.

"I didn't want to mention it for obvious reasons," he went on. "I'm sorry I upset you."

"No, I asked you about your hobbies. You shouldn't change your answer just because of—"

"It's just that—" he said at the same time. He motioned for her to go on, but she shook her head.

He looked uncomfortable, and Ren regretted the turn in their conversation. There was no way she could go back now, so she waited for Jonas's confession.

"It's what Kai and I did together," he said. "We both liked to scuba dive, and we went out in the water all the time."

"You went in the lake?" Ren asked. "I had wondered if it was really deep enough."

He nodded. "Yeah. It's deepest just beyond your dock."

Ren gave an involuntary shiver. Jonas was looking at his feet, so he didn't see it.

They were quiet for a long moment. Ren didn't know what to say, so she let Jonas come up with the next topic of conversation.

"That friend of yours is really something," he said, scratching the back of his neck.

"He's my best friend," Ren told him.

"That's the way I felt about Kai," he returned.

He let out a long breath. "I keep doing that, don't I?"

"It's okay," Ren assured him. "I think about him a lot, too."

"You don't wear your wedding band anymore," he pointed out.

Ren lifted her left hand and surveyed the finger that had sported a wedding band and engagement ring for four years. "I stopped wearing it a couple of months ago. I only had the engagement ring. I put my wedding band in the casket with him."

"You don't say his name."

Jonas measured her with his eyes, and she was struck by his appearance in the twilight. Suddenly, she wanted his strong arms around her. If they weren't talking about her dead husband, Ren would have kissed him.

"Can we talk about something else?"

"We probably should," he agreed.

Ren strained to think about safe conversations, but Jonas beat her to it. "Do you like ice cream?"

Her mouth twitched at the corners. The woodsy man beside her was asking if she liked a childhood treat.

"Yes."

He pulled an arm loosely over her shoulders as they walked to his truck. "There's a great little shack on the other side of the lake. They sell homemade ice cream to the tourists, but the locals like it, too."

Ren enjoyed his closeness, and she imagined what it would feel like to have both of his arms wrapped around her again. She didn't press the issue, though. Jonas wanted to take things slowly, and she needed to be careful with her heart and with him.

CHAPTER 16

"**G**ood morning, sunshine!"

"You're up early," Ren remarked, handing him a cup of coffee. She had just finished lunch, but she'd kept the pot of coffee on for her friend.

Gonzo yawned and stretched. "I got into bed early. Or I guess I did. I woke up in the bed with my clothes on, so I must have been pretty smashed."

"It didn't look like you had a lot of wine," Ren said. "I was surprised you didn't wait up for me."

"I may have dipped into the liquor cabinet," Gonzo admitted.

"There's a liquor cabinet?" Ren asked.

Gonzo put his feet up on the table. He had taken a shower, but Ren was a little perturbed by the action.

"Yeah. It's under the desk in the office."

Ren shook her head. "It was locked."

Gonzo pointed at her. "*Was* is the key word. No wonder there are so many drunk teenagers. That was one of the easiest locks I've ever picked."

"And we still can't get the basement door open."

Gonzo jumped up. "I can try it again, but it's more about brute force than locks, and I" —he held up his spindly arms— "am not going to get it open."

Before Ren could object, Gonzo ran to the basement door. He pressed himself against it.

"Maybe it would give if we both pushed it."

Ren leveled her body and grabbed the handle. They both pushed, and the door gave way.

An undefinable smell reached her nose, and Ren almost gagged. "What is that?"

"It's probably a dead animal," Gonzo said.

He placed a foot on the first step, and when it seemed sturdy, he bounced down the steps into the darkness.

"Wait!" Ren called after him. "I need to get a flashlight."

She ran to the drawer that held the flashlights and emergency kits. She grabbed the first one she saw and joined Gonzo.

Gonzo pushed her flashlight down. "Turn it off. You can see everything down here when your eyes adjust."

Ren remembered seeing a window on the back side of the house and determined that it must stream enough light to help them see.

A scratching noise followed by a bang echoed against the concrete walls, and Ren screamed. Gonzo put his arm around her waist.

"It's okay, Rennie. I'll go check it out."

Ren couldn't open her mouth to object, but every fiber in her being yelled against the steps Gonzo took as he made his way toward the source of the sound. He crept softly, not wanting to disturb the wild animal. The sound repeated, coming from a space behind the furnace. Just as Gonzo moved to the side, the sound issued more forcefully than the other two times.

Gonzo squealed and bolted up the stairs, dragging Ren with him. "Whatever it is, can stay down there!" he said, slamming the basement door shut. "Screw that!"

Urgent knocking caused them both to cry out. Ren's hand went to her chest, but she was the first one to recover and answered the door.

Jonas stood on the porch, panting. "I heard screaming."

"From your house?"

It took him a moment to answer. Ren wasn't sure if he was going to lie to her or if he was simply catching his breath.

"I was out for a run, and this is part of the path I take."

Ren looked skeptically at his jeans and tee shirt. She didn't think of them as running clothes, but he was wearing a pair of sneakers, and he'd always worn boots on their dates.

"We heard something in the basement, and when we went to check on it—"

"You went into the basement!" he interrupted. "There are snakes and who knows what other wild animals down there."

"We didn't see whatever it was, but it must be in pain."

Jonas brushed by her and went down the basement stairs, opening the door as easily as if he did it every day. Gonzo stared after him but showed no signs of following. Whatever had inspired him had diminished when he'd almost met the wild animal in the basement.

Minutes ticked by, and the friends settled on the couch together. They were silent, straining their ears for whatever was happening in the basement.

Thirty minutes later, Jonas returned, but he came through the front door and shut the basement up firmly.

"I've taken care of the problem," he announced and headed back to the front door.

"Hey," Ren called after him. When she and Gonzo caught up to him, she asked, "What was it?"

"It was a bear cub," he told them gruffly. "It must have gotten in through one of the high windows and broken its hip when it fell. I put it out of its misery and locked the windows."

Ren and Gonzo gasped.

"You say you got rid of it," Ren said, "but I didn't see you bring it up."

"I took it out the basement door," he replied, clenching his jaw. "Next time, I'll bring it upstairs for your approval."

His harsh words stung Ren. She'd thought they were growing closer, but Jonas wasn't even treating her like a friend. Gonzo noticed her withdrawal, and he swooped in with his good humor to save her any more embarrassment.

"Well, it's a good thing we had a big, strong man like you around to save the day."

Jonas measured Gonzo, and when he asserted Gonzo was sincere, he smiled. "It won't bother you anymore."

"That poor bear," Ren groaned miserably.

Jonas spat in the other direction. Ren thought it was disgusting, and she couldn't remember him doing it any other time.

"It's better off," he responded coolly and walked away, his feet hitting the ground in rapid steps.

He picked up a shovel at the end of the path and carried it with him. Ren hoped he'd dragged the bear into the woods to bury it and she wouldn't see the grave of the poor animal when she roamed her property.

"That was weird," Gonzo commented when they were back inside the house.

They discussed the experience as Ren made blueberry pancakes. They couldn't let the subject of the heart-stopping event go until Gonzo took his first bite.

"How do you make these so good?" he groaned. "It's like they almost melt in my mouth."

"I make them *so well* because I take the time to measure ingredients and I put the stove on medium heat."

Gonzo had prepared one meal for Ren, and it had been a disaster. The bread had been darkened to a crisp, and the salad dripped with oil.

Gonzo chose to ignore her slight on his cooking and focused on the insult to his grammar. "Maybe if you're so concerned about my speech, you should try hopping on your laptop and writing."

"I wrote a little yesterday."

Gonzo shook his head. "Those two little sentences won't finish the book. At that rate, you'll be finishing it up when my grandchildren are in college."

"Does that mean you've decided to pop the question?" Ren asked, startling him.

"I, uh, I— I don't know."

"You're considering it?" Ren pressed.

"You're making it hard for me to finish my pancakes."

"Can't you talk and eat?" she joked. "You never had trouble with it before."

Gonzo stared at his plate of syrupy breakfast, and Ren regretted putting so much pressure on him. He would have told her about his intentions as he started to accept them, but she was curious. Just as she was about to apologize, he looked up with a crooked smile.

"Do you want to help me look at some rings?"

Chapter 17

"I didn't think you'd want to take me out tonight after what happened earlier."

A look of irritation passed over Jonas's face, but it was gone as quickly as the clouds swept across the moon. "I'm sorry about my actions."

Ren didn't want to waste her time with someone whose mood could vary by the hour. "Why do you act that way? That wasn't the first time, and honestly, I'm tired of it."

They'd been sitting on the tailgate of his truck. Jonas had brought a couple of blankets, but they'd shared the biggest one as they stared up at the stars. Ren felt his body shift away from her as he sat up, and she held the blanket more tightly to herself.

Ren liked both ways he fixed his hair, sometimes brushed back and other times with a rigid part, but she favored the times when it was brushed back. It revealed more of his forehead, and the lines that popped up when they had serious talks made him seem more human and vulnerable.

"I don't know what gets into me," he said, throwing his hands up. "I guess I'm just not used to people."

"Don't you talk to anyone who lives around the lake?"

"Sometimes." He turned his face up to the sky. "But it's mostly just my brother and me, and we avoid each other a lot of the time."

The pity Ren felt for him only went so far. "You're going to have to find a way to deal with it if this is going to work," she told him. "I'm tired of the hot-and-cold attitude."

She almost felt like she was scolding a child. Jonas seemed miserable, so she decided to have mercy on him.

"I think it's time for me to go home."

He jerked to attention and grabbed her hands. She hadn't noticed how cold they were until his warm hand encircled them.

"Please don't go yet," he begged. "I don't want you to leave before I have the chance to make it up to you."

He was so sincere that Ren couldn't deny his request. She doubted he could do anything to make her feel better about their relationship, as she planned to end it the following day. It was proving to be too much for her, and Gonzo's idea about a fling seemed way more appealing than dealing with emotional baggage.

"Collette slept with my brother," he said, and Ren was sucked back in.

"What?"

The shadow of his profile fell as he dipped his head. Ren waited for whatever he was willing to reveal.

"I should have known what he was trying to do when he sent me to pick up food, but I trusted them."

"You walked in on them?" The words tumbled out before she could stop them.

He grimaced. "Not exactly. Whatever they had done, they did just before I got there. But Collette's hair was messy, and there was a smell in the air."

Ren's mouth formed a thin line. She didn't know what to say.

"I was pretty attached to her," he went on. "I may have even loved her, so I laid it out for them. I let my temper get the best of me, and my brother walked around with a swollen lip for two weeks."

"You never saw them together, though?"

Jonas's head popped up, and he stared at her. Dark shadows fell across his face, but his touch was warm, and his tone was sad.

"They admitted it."

Ren was almost certain Jonas was crying, and when she reached for him, her suspicions were confirmed. She held him until his lips were on hers, with nothing watching them but the stars.

"You had sex!" Gonzo shouted as soon as she entered the house.

Ren had hoped he'd be sleeping or in his room, but he had waited for her in the living room, with a glass of wine beside him and his phone face down on his lap. She straightened her posture and joined him, admitting nothing.

Gonzo turned to face her fully, crossing his legs in front of him. "How was it?"

"It was fine."

The smile that had spread across his face dropped. "Fine? We're not talking about your latest experience at the local supermarket. I want to know if he made your toes curl."

"Gonzo!" Ren admonished, swatting a hand at her friend.

"You get embarrassed over the strangest things," he remarked. "It's just sex."

"I've not really talked about it before," Ren admitted.

"Well, let me help you through this difficult time." He narrowed his eyes mischievously. "Length? Girth?"

Ren jumped up. "I am not having this conversation!" She felt the color rise to her cheeks, but she was privately amused.

Gonzo threw his head back on the couch. "You have to give me something, Rennie!"

Ren sat back down on the couch. "There's not a lot to tell. He was crying, and I wanted to make him feel better."

Gonzo let out a sound between a yell and a sigh of exasperation. "Pity sex? You haven't been with anyone since your husband died, and your first time was to make someone *else* feel better?"

"I like him," Ren countered. "I was going to do it the night before you got here."

"And I would have fully supported that," Gonzo said. "You've been someone's emotional doormat for too long."

Ren's eyebrows drew together. "What's that supposed to mean?"

Gonzo softened his voice. "Look, I know he was good to you, but after the accident—"

"Stop," she warned.

He sucked his bottom lip in and out. "I love you, and I want something better for you than an introverted country bumpkin."

"I'm a rural introvert." Her voice was hardly a whisper.

Gonzo put his arm around her. "And that's the reason you need someone to balance you. Kai was good for a while, but he changed."

Ren wanted to do anything but think about what Gonzo had implied, but her mind kept going back to it, and late in the night, within the stillness of her dreams, she returned to her doomed anniversary.

CHAPTER 18

I t was clear Kai was too drunk to drive.

Ren waited for him to fumble with his keys and deliberately place one into the ignition. She finally spoke up when he missed the buckle for his seatbelt three times.

"Should we hire a driver?"

He stopped fidgeting with the radio and stared at her. "That would be expensive, and I don't want to leave my car so far away. Why do we need one, anyway?"

Because you're going to wreck the car you love so much with me in it, Ren thought. She said, "We've had so much fun tonight, and it's our anniversary. If someone else drove us home, we could get a head start on—" She whispered her intentions in his ear.

"That sounds like fun," Kai said, licking his lips. "Let me get us home so we can start."

Ren looked down at her hands. Usually, she wasn't a religious person, but she prayed they would make it home in one piece.

Cool temperatures still lingered, and the sun's disappearance made the day cooler. The clouds covered the sky, and even though the sun would set in another hour, it was dark.

Kai navigated Asheville's busy streets and the cloverleaf on the interstate without difficulty, but once he was on a straighter, less populated part of the highway, he grew less concerned about remaining alert. At one point, cars breezed by him, while the BMW cruised along at thirty-five miles per hour.

Ren tried to get him to pull over and get a hotel room. She used every female wile in her artillery, but Kai insisted he needed to go to work the next day and that his car shouldn't be left out in a parking lot overnight.

His eyebrows stayed low, and his mouth turned down into a constant frown. Ren was used to the change in his attitude after too much alcohol. She had learned that Kai could drink steadily and remain social and polite, but once the beer or wine stopped flowing, he had an hour before sleepiness would set in and he'd get bitey.

She thought she could soften the situation by seducing him into pulling over. After sex, he might be more likely to fall asleep, and she could set her phone to wake them up in the morning. He might be angry with her for it, but it would stop him from weaving from the middle of the road to the shoulder.

She unbuckled her seatbelt and put her mouth to his ear, letting her warm breath travel down his neck. No sooner had she touched his zipper, than he swatted away her hand.

"Stop it, Lauren!" He moved in his seat to make himself less accessible. "And put your seatbelt back on. You're going to get us pulled over."

Ren obliged and crossed her arms over her chest. She was out of options, so the only thing left for her to do was to try to keep her husband awake until they arrived home.

Kai adjusted the radio again. He could control it from his steering wheel, but his fingers kept sliding off the buttons. He took his eyes off the road and squinted at the screen, attempting to move the radio back to another favored channel.

"Can I see if there's anything that I like?" Ren asked sweetly.

He glared at her and threw up his hand, but he motioned for her to make a selection. She was careful to pick songs he liked, even though they had different tastes in music.

The state line whipped past them, and Kai put more pressure on the gas. He believed that no law officers waited in the medians in Tennessee, but Ren knew better. She had seen many people pulled over by state troopers who had thought they were safe when North Carolina was in their rearview mirror.

The dips between one side of the road to the other were much more noticeable as Kai increased his speed. Ren wondered if it wouldn't be better for them to be pulled over. Kai could probably argue himself out of a DUI charge, as he knew most of the officers in the area, but the officer would have to take them home or to jail.

Ren had grown increasingly nervous over their drive, and after Kai nearly clipped a guardrail, her anxiety heightened to an almost uncontrollable level. She nearly vibrated with nervous energy, and the effects of the champagne left her body.

"Can I drive?" she blurted.

"What's wrong with you?" Kai shouted. "Don't you trust me to get us home?"

"Yes," Ren answered, attempting to placate him. "But it's a nice night, and I thought I could drive for a little while."

"You never ask to drive the car," he pointed out. "You don't think I should be driving?" His knuckles tightened over the wheel. "Say it."

"What do you want me to say?"

"Say that you don't trust me to get us home," he barked.

Ren jumped in her seat, and he smiled. She tried to keep her voice calm, even though she wanted to be anywhere but in the car with her husband. He had never acted so harshly with her, and Ren was more frightened than angry.

"I trust you."

"You trust me to what?" He clenched his teeth and pushed down on the gas.

Recognizing his action as a threat, Ren hurried to remedy the situation. "I trust you to drive us home. I'm sorry I asked to drive the car."

He didn't respond to her, but he sat a little straighter, a self-satisfied smile inching across his face.

Ren counted down the minutes until the car would pull into the driveway. She reasoned they were less than twenty minutes from home, so she started counting back from fifteen minutes.

Kai reached over and started pushing the radio's screen. "I don't like anything they're playing tonight. How can I make up with you properly when I can't find a decent love song?" He looked over at her with gently lidded eyes.

Ren felt her heart soften, and she asked his permission to scan the stations. While she was trying to find a song, a horn blared. Ren looked up, and Kai had his eyes closed.

She yelled his name, and he popped to attention. "I'm fine," he said. "We'll be home in a few minutes."

Ren was too scared to argue with him, so she went back to trying to find a suitable station. She felt a hard bump, and it jarred her.

Ren glanced over at her husband slumped over the wheel, and she had enough time to see the guardrail whiz by on their left side. Paralyzed with fear, Ren was unable to pull her husband's foot off the gas or try to steer the car away from the embankment.

Ren was fully awake as the car slammed into a patch of boulders and went airborne. When the car hit the water, her world went dark. She woke up underwater.

CHAPTER 19

R en slept a lot longer than usual.

When she woke, she stripped the sheets off her bed and took a shower. On her way downstairs, she smelled coffee and heard snatches of chatter.

"But it is the best restaurant in the city."

"Well, this Friday, my friend is going to open a place that will blow your socks off!"

The talking stopped when she entered the kitchen, carrying a pile of sheets in front of her. Ren stared at Becky and Gonzo as they sat at the table, smiling up at her.

"Good morning, sunshine," Gonzo said. "You slept later than me today." He motioned at the sheets. "But now I see why."

Becky's head whipped around. "Why?" she asked him.

"She's purging," he said nonchalantly, taking a drink from Ren's favorite mug.

"Purging?" Becky questioned.

"Yeah. It's what you do when you feel guilty about sleeping with someone." He pointed to the sheets in her arms. "She's gonna wash sheets she didn't use in the act and maybe clean all the shiny surfaces in the house."

Becky looked at him in awe. "How do you know that?"

"I may have a little experience," he admitted. "I threw out all my CDs once because one was playing while I—"

Ren dropped her sheets on the floor. "Yes. We get it. While you were doing any number of debaucheries." She took the mug out of his hand and threw the contents into the sink, but the smug smile never left his face.

A light seemed to go off in Becky's eyes. "If you didn't do it in your bed, where *did* you do it?"

Gonzo put his finger to his chin and adopted the air of a professional. "It's my guess, given Jonas's cowboy boots and slicked-back hair, they did the deed in the back of his pickup truck."

Ren colored, and it was the only confirmation he needed. "Well, giddy up, little doggies, I was right!"

"You shouldn't talk that way," Ren said. "It's not nice."

He flicked his finger against the placemat. "I'm sure you'll make it up to him if I hurt his little feelings." He turned out his bottom lip.

Ren rolled her eyes.

"Did I miss something?" Becky asked.

"Rennie only slept with the cowboy next door because she felt sorry for him."

Ren could see Becky assessing the value of the information. Soon, she'd be sharing the gossip with the local lake people. Ren could ask her to keep it to herself, and Becky would swear herself to secrecy, but she'd spill everything she'd heard as soon as she came in contact with another person. All Ren could do was try to keep Gonzo from saying anything more.

Becky tilted her head. "Oh... But it was still good, right?"

Gonzo leaned forward conspiratorially. "She said it was *fine*." He put air quotes around the word.

Becky pressed her lips together and nodded. She cast a pitying look at Ren.

"I'm sorry," she said. "You'd think with his looks, deep voice, and mysterious personality—"

"I'm finished talking about it," Ren shot back, a little louder than she'd intended.

Becky recoiled, but Gonzo only lifted his eyebrows. He shook a finger in her direction.

"Calm down. We're only having a little fun."

He had blabbed about her personal experience with a gossipy neighbor, but it wasn't because he valued Becky or her opinions. Gonzo wanted to get Ren out of her shell, and even though he did it by embarrassing her in front of others, his loyalty remained true to her.

He crossed the room and threw an arm over her shoulder. "You're so serious."

Ren slouched into his embrace and forgave him easily. Sure, her love life would be a popular subject of conversation in the community, but she didn't really know those people.

But Gonzo wasn't finished with his gentle ribbing. "Leave me alone with Jonas for a few minutes, and you'll never have to worry about mediocre sex again."

Ren playfully swatted him, and Becky almost choked on her coffee.

"I'm sorry about last night," Jonas said.

Ren smiled over her pizza. "There's nothing to apologize for."

He reached across the table and took her hand. "I should never have unloaded on you."

Ren looked at their hands and moved her thumb along his palm. "It's okay. I'm glad you trust me."

She had intended to end her relationship with Jonas when he picked her up, but his smile had been so genuine and unencumbered that she continued their date. She was almost certain Gonzo had laughed to himself as he watched them leave, knowing she had backed out of her original plan.

"I haven't really taken it slow," he observed, raising his eyebrows at her.

"No, I guess not."

"Is that okay?"

Now was her chance to ease out of any future commitments. She could propose that they go back to a friendly status and laugh about her eager hormones. She opened her mouth to voice her feelings, but Jonas spoke.

"I trust you," he said. "I haven't felt this way in a long time, and I hope you know you can trust me, too."

Ren felt all her hope for pulling out of the relationship diminish. She squeezed his hand and looked forward to another time when she could end things easily.

"The conquering hero returns to her abode!" Gonzo announced as she stumbled into the living room.

Ren fumbled for a light, and finding none, she plopped onto the floor. Gonzo got up and helped her to her feet.

"Another night of disappointing sex?"

"I don't know," Ren slurred.

"Well, I hope you know whether he used protection."

Ren glared at him. "I made sure of it. I don't want to be saddled with him for eighteen years." She laughed at her unintentional joke and attempted to get a chuckle out of her friend. "You know, *saddled*? Because you call him a cowboy."

"Uh-huh. I think it's time to get you upstairs."

"Yes," she agreed. "But there aren't any sheets on the bed."

He smoothed the hair back from her face. "I took care of it while you were gone."

They stopped at the bathroom, and Gonzo grabbed a wastebasket. He carried it with them and placed it beside the bed.

Instead of leaving her and going to his room, Gonzo removed her shoes and jeans and covered her with a sheet. He laid down behind her and curled his arm around her waist.

"This is nice," Ren said.

"Don't get any ideas," he joked. "I'm taken."

"I wouldn't dream of it."

She fell asleep, wondering how she'd landed herself in her current relationship. She had been good at picking all her other partners, and she thought Kai had been her best choice. Until the accident, he had been the closest thing to perfection.

CHAPTER 20

The bright sun insisted she open her eyes.

"Good morning, my love," Kai told her. "Can I make you some breakfast?"

She took one look at his dark, gently tussled hair and even smile, and she wanted to crawl under the bed. There was no way that she looked as good as him in the morning.

"Bacon and eggs?"

He scrunched up his nose. "How about blueberry pancakes and a mimosa?"

Her stomach rumbled at the thought. With a smile, Kai hopped off the bed and headed downstairs to cook.

Ren's suspicions about her appearance were confirmed when she half-stumbled to the bathroom. Her mascara and eyeliner were nonexistent on one eye and smeared on the other. She ran back to the bedroom and rejoiced when she located her overnight bag. She'd started bringing it with her after she and Kai had been together for a month.

She took a shower and applied her makeup, carefully winging her eyeliner. When she walked into the kitchen, Kai whistled.

"You look like a dream."

Even though they'd been together for a couple of months, he could still make her blush. Ren was aware most men found her attractive, but she sought to remain humble about it. When Kai spoke to her, though, she wanted to return his charisma with an ego she didn't possess.

He kissed her and excused himself to take a shower. When he returned, Ren had eaten the three pancakes he'd left for her.

"Wow! You have a big appetite." He stared at her seriously. "I hope that doesn't mean you're eating for two."

She shook her head. They'd already talked about children, and neither of them was interested in parenthood.

"Are you ready for an adventure?" he asked.

She looked up at him, ready for whatever he had to say. Kai always made plans for their time together, and Ren had been surprised by how much she enjoyed everything he had suggested.

"I thought we could take a little trip to the ocean," he revealed. "I was going to surprise you with it, but since we'll be gone a couple of days, I thought you might like to pick up some things before we leave."

Ren popped out of her chair. "I love the ocean!"

He was thrown off by her exuberance, but happy she was excited about his plans. They were ready to go in less than an hour, as Ren had put together a bag quickly when they had stopped at her apartment. She knew exactly what she needed to maximize her time at the beach.

It took them almost six hours to reach the nearest shore, but once they got there, they both felt infused with life. Ren thought the air was fresher, and the sun was brighter.

"Even though it's a holiday weekend, the crowds should be low where we're going," Kai said.

He pulled into a gated community with homes along the beachfront. Ren's mouth fell open as she took in the pricey homes, and Kai pulled his BMW into the driveway of one of the most sizeable houses.

"A client owed me a favor, so—"

Ren didn't hear the rest of what he said because she was already out of the car. She ran to the water, stripping her clothes to reveal the bikini she'd put on at her house.

When her body hit the ocean, she felt alive. The water caressed her skin like a well-known lover, and the smell of saltwater made every sense more alert.

Kai stood on the shore laughing at her. "I didn't think you'd go swimming as soon as you got out of the car."

She threw her hands up as she trod water. She swam as he opened up the house. She was certain it was lovely, but she had no desire to tour the rooms while she could enjoy the ocean.

Homes lined up on each side of the house, and families played on the sand. She liked to hear squeals of delight from the children, and she was happy she wasn't responsible for their safety. The ocean and the rest of the world were dangerous, and it was hard enough to protect herself against the cruelties of humankind.

Kai joined her in the water, and after a spirited swim, they lay on beach towels. A cabana sat above them, but there was something about the warmth of the sand beneath her towel that relaxed Ren in a way that wasn't possible for an outdoor shelter from the sun.

Kai rubbed sunscreen across her exposed flesh, and she wondered how a man could be so perfect for her. He deepened that feeling with his next suggestion.

"I have reservations for dinner, but later on, I've made plans for us to go scuba diving."

Ren lifted her upper body off the towel. "At night?"

"Yes," he said. "They're different—"

Ren didn't let him finish. She kissed him and said, "My dad used to take me scuba diving all the time. I love going at night!"

Once he realized Ren's eagerness to get on the water, Kai canceled the dinner reservation. They grabbed a quick dinner at the closest fast-food restaurant, and Kai drove them to a small structure on an otherwise abandoned shore. The building didn't have a sign, but there were two surfboards painted on either side of the entrance.

An unusually tall man with salt and pepper hair and weathered skin was teaching a class to two couples. When he saw them, he handed over the instruction to a blonde woman who did not look like she was ready to go into the water with her heavily drawn face and too-tight pink dress.

The man shook Kai's hand. "Wilson Caruthers."

"Kai Martin," Kai returned. "And this is my girlfriend, Lauren."

"Ren," she corrected, but both men only assumed it was a nickname.

"We spoke on the phone about a night dive," Kai prompted.

"Yes, I remember." He jerked a thumb in Ren's direction. "I've seen your card, but can you assure me she has the proper experience?"

"Yes," he replied. "She used to dive with her family, but they never took official classes."

Ren shot him a questioning look.

Kai scratched the back of his head. "I may have called your dad about it."

Ren smiled and addressed the instructor. "Mr. Caruthers—"

"Wilson."

"Okay, Wilson. I have spent many hours underwater during the day and night. My father's favorite time to dive was in the evening, just before sunset. He thought it helped his eyes adjust better."

Wilson gave her an appreciating look. "He was exactly right, and that's what we plan to do today. I don't usually allow anyone on my boat until they've passed the classes, but Kai is a good friend of a man I'd trust with my life, so I'll let your possible inexperience slide." He pointed a finger at her. "But if you give me a reason to doubt your abilities, I will pull you out of the water myself."

Ren and Kai sat through the final instructions and followed Wilson onto a rigid-hulled inflatable boat. A stout man with a cigarette dangling from his lips steered the boat while Wilson shouted about the sights. Once they stopped, a young boy helped Wilson suit up the divers. Wilson looked even taller in his suit, and Ren could almost imagine the rigid muscles beneath it.

Wilson was a good instructor, and Ren trusted his expertise. He boasted twenty dives a week—and those were only his personal dives. He was kind, but the firmness behind his tone let everyone know he expected his directions to be followed to the letter.

The sun touched the horizon and glittered on the water. A bird squawked overhead, but Ren's eyes focused on Kai.

"Thank you for doing this," she said.

"I was happy to do it. After all, we missed our lake date."

Ren stared out at the expanse of the ocean. "This certainly makes up for it."

Even though there was light left in the sky, Wilson told them to enter the water with their feet first. "It may be a little darker under the surface," he explained. "You could feel some vertigo if we dove backward."

Ren was the first one in the water. She adjusted her strobe light and took in the surrounding scene.

A few fish were swimming in the distance, but what stood out to her the most was silence. Her moment was interrupted when her diving buddy, Kai, joined her in the water. Soon, Wilson, the young boy, and the two other couples joined them.

Wilson guided them using basic hand signals, and when darkness surrounded them, he used a light to communicate. Ren wasn't as concerned with the ocean life as she was with feeling her weightlessness in the water. If she'd had it her way, she would be the only one floating in the dark water, oblivious to the rest of the world.

Too soon, the experience was over. Everyone, even Kai, was alive with the sights they'd witnessed, but Ren was deflated. She wished for nothing more than to be back in the ocean alone.

Ren had never been suicidal, so she didn't want to sink into the ocean's depths, but the stillness had consumed her. When she'd first entered the water, she'd been alone. No one expected anything from her. She wasn't obligated to be social or live up to the expectations of others.

Ren stared out at the ocean as a tear rolled down her cheek. She swiped at it, flinging it into the water.

"What's wrong, my love?" Kai asked.

Ren plastered on a smile. "It was just so beautiful."

"I know," he agreed. "Did you see the—"

Ren tuned him out and smiled and nodded as he talked about his observations. She wore a mask of amusement as he spoke until they got back to the house.

They showered separately, and Ren cried, keeping her sobs low. She didn't trust the acoustics in an unknown place.

Kai's enthusiasm after their showers showed he hadn't heard her cries. As she lay beneath him, Ren both loved and hated him. He had given her a beautiful experience, but that experience had awakened a desire she'd never known, and now Ren knew what she was missing. And she didn't plan to live without it.

CHAPTER 21

R en rolled over and groaned. The light hurt her eyes, and Gonzo had forgotten to close the shades before he climbed into bed next to her.

He had elected to throw a pillow over his head. The occasional twitches in his arms and legs indicated he was cold, so Ren pulled her sheet over him.

She grabbed her clothes and tiptoed to the shower. She kept the towel on her wet hair as she prepared coffee.

The doorbell chimed, and Ren looked at the clock on the stove. It was a few minutes before noon, and that was a time Becky had been known to visit.

Ren grudgingly opened the door, and a man on her porch holding long-stemmed roses in a vase surprised her. She relieved the delivery man of his burden and brought them to her nose. She didn't have to look at the card to know they were from Jonas.

She read the card but placed it back in the envelope. She stared at the flowers and remembered Kai's romantic gestures.

Her husband had bought her jewelry, chocolates, and flowers. He had taken her on expensive trips, and they had dined in the best restaurants. Aside from the attention he lavishly bestowed on her, Ren was happy with him. When they were together, she and Kai could agree on movies to watch and who should perform certain household chores. Kai understood her insecurities, and even though he sought to bring her around more people, he would back off when it was clear she needed time to herself.

Jonas was new and a little exciting, but he didn't act like Kai. Sure, he paid for their meals and had purchased the vase of long-stemmed beauties in front of her, but he hadn't taken the time to get to know her. If he had, he would have sent carnations and baby's breath.

Jonas had asked her some of the usual questions, like her favorite music and where she had gone to school, but when it came to more intimate questions, he had only focused on himself. Ren knew way more about him than he knew about her.

Before she'd met Kai, Ren never would have let herself fall into that type of relationship. Maybe the difference in her attitude had to do with living with a person who met her needs physically and emotionally.

Of course, it wasn't true during the last year of her marriage. The last eight months she'd spent with Kai had been the hardest, and she tried to block them out. They wouldn't listen, though, and they floated to the surface of her mind, obliterating her peace.

CHAPTER 22

R en's eyes opened underwater.

At first, there was the feeling of peace she always felt when she dove into the lake or ocean, but then her need to breathe caught up with her. She wasn't fully aware of how she'd ended up in her position, and when she looked over, she saw Kai slumped against a steering wheel.

She flew into action. Kai's seatbelt unbuckled easily, and his body floated to the top of the cab, bending at an awkward angle. She tried to open his door or roll down his window, but after she managed to unbuckle her safety belt, the water's pressure prevented her from opening the door, and the automatic windows wouldn't budge.

Her brain raced to find a solution, landing on the spring-loaded window breaker she had seen in his glove box. The glove box came open, and her lungs screamed for air as she frantically searched the compartment.

Her face and neck felt pressured, and she lost hope. With her last bit of energy, she banged on the car window and stabbed the button that controlled it.

Water encircled her on all sides, lifting her hair around her face and weighing her down. She lost the will to push against it.

Isn't this what she'd always wanted? She had felt at home in the water and had almost begged to remain in its depths. Now, she could have her wish.

Ren's throat burned.

A cup was thrust into her hand, and medical personnel asked soft questions. She could only stare at them, as her mind hadn't caught up with her surroundings enough to answer them. She phased into her awareness as she sat at the end of an ambulance. The night was dark beyond the blinding lights of the emergency vehicles, and the headlights from passing cars momentarily blinded her until she looked at the river that had almost claimed her life.

It was the second time that night she had woken into something that felt like a dream. If her throat hadn't been on fire, Ren would have settled into the blanket around her and embraced unconsciousness. She blinked, and someone shook her.

"I'm going to need you to stay awake, honey," a male voice said.

She was outraged by the endearment. Only her husband was allowed to—

Where was Kai?

She echoed her thoughts to the emergency crew around her. They stared at each other, as if debating whether to tell her about his fate.

"Where is my husband?" she spoke more firmly. She was rewarded with a coughing fit.

Once she had taken a drink of water to soothe her throat, a woman explained. "They've already loaded him in a separate ambulance, and he's on the way to the hospital." She paused, pressing her plump lips together before continuing. "It doesn't look good."

"Is she okay?" a man's voice asked.

The emergency crew parted, and a man with dripping blond hair and gold-rimmed glasses approached her. His shirt and shoes seemed to be dry, but his tight pants clung even more to his skin.

"She'll have to be examined, but she's fine for now," the woman told him.

The man backed away a step until he noticed Ren looking at him. "I thought you were dead."

Tears made tracks down his cheeks. *Or was it water?* Ren decided it didn't matter. It was obvious he had pulled her from the river.

"Thank you," she croaked, feeling the pain in her throat more acutely.

The man nodded. "I'm sorry I didn't get to your husband. I had to try to get the water out of your lungs."

Ren didn't ask what he meant. Instead, she repeated her appreciation, and the man moved away. The man to her left grabbed a blanket from a drawer in the ambulance and chased after him.

Ren shivered, and once it started, she couldn't seem to control it. No matter how many blankets they threw around her, she continued to shake.

She begged to see Kai, but the only answer she received was a benign smile from the female who stayed with her until her ambulance arrived at the hospital.

It was days before she saw her husband again, and when she did, he wasn't the same.

Chapter 23

"**A**re those from the cowboy?" Gonzo asked, momentarily cupping a bud.

Ren nodded. "He's trying too hard."

"Obviously," Gonzo agreed.

His lips moved as he read the card. "I thought you said he wanted to take it slow. At this rate, you'll be married by Christmas."

"Gonzo!"

He raised his eyebrows and put the card in front of the vase. "He'll be by to see you today." He tapped the card. "You need to make it look like you've been reading that over and over."

His tone wasn't as humorous as usual. He poured himself a cup of coffee and sat opposite the roses.

"What do you mean?" Ren asked.

He took a sip of coffee, savoring the taste, and gulped. "He's going to see if you're really into him."

"I thought the sex made it obvious."

Gonzo laughed. "No. Sex is sex. Your cowboy has some feelings for you, and he wants to see if you like him, too."

It was uncharacteristic for Gonzo to be so serious. She couldn't help asking him about it.

Gonzo pushed his mug to the length of his arms. "He's not good for you."

He didn't explain his assessment or offer her a solution to the problem he'd presented. Ren had considered it, but hearing Gonzo say the words confirmed her feelings.

"How do I end it, though," she said. "Every time I try, he comes up with a sob story, and I can't let him down."

"Leave," Gonzo said. "You don't owe him anything. Leave the house and sell it. You won't ever have to see him again."

"But I haven't gone through all the stuff—"

"And you won't," Gonzo interrupted. "You'll never be finished with this house or the one you live in because they're the last links you have to—"

"I can do it," Ren shouted.

Gonzo was stricken, but he quickly recovered. "Then do it. I'll hold off the cowboy until you're finished, and we'll leave tonight."

Ren considered his idea. There was one thing she'd planned to do while she was at the lake house, but she'd have to do it somewhere else. It had felt like the right place, though, and she was upset as she wondered if she could ever find the nerve to go through with it in another place.

"Okay."

Gonzo looked up, clearly surprised. "Really?"

"Yeah. I need to get out of here."

"I can only imagine."

"I shouldn't feel that way," she said. "I don't get upset where we used to live."

"Is that so? Why haven't you gotten any writing done?"

"It's distracting there," she admitted, "but I don't feel like he's around every corner."

"I can understand that."

Ren's eyebrows drew together. "You can?"

"Sure," he replied. "You're close to the water when you're here. And that was the last place—"

"I better get started," she said, keeping him from traveling down a line of conversation she avoided.

She set to work in the living room, gathering dusty photographs and family memories. She found a Bible that had somewhat of a family genealogy, and her name was listed in the mix of relatives. She ran her finger over the date she'd married Kai.

It had been a beach wedding, and her hair had whipped in the wind as she said her vows. Kai's eyes never left her as he recited the lines after the preacher.

She didn't realize she'd been crying until Gonzo's arm was around her. He held her, and they rocked until her tears subsided.

"I knew it would be hard," she told him.

He brushed a strand of hair from her sweaty forehead. "That's why you avoided it for so long." He took a deep breath and looked around them. "But this is not your place—even though you own it. It's a tomb of memories."

Gonzo could be profound when he wasn't trying to make himself the life of the party. Ren cherished her private moments with him when they were truly themselves.

She held up the Bible. "His parents marked the day we were married."

Gonzo looked at it and scrunched his nose. "His middle name was Egbert?"

Ren sighed. "It's a regal name."

"Whatever you say, but I wouldn't want the first syllable of my name to have egg in it."

"What's Blane's middle name?" she asked, hoping to veer the conversation away from Kai. She hadn't expected his hair-trigger response.

"Geoffery."

"That's really nice."

Gonzo leaned against a nearby chair. "It is, isn't it?"

Ren took one look at the faraway stare in his eyes, and she knew Gonzo was hooked. "You love him."

She almost expected him to deny it or cover his feelings with humor, but Gonzo replied. "Yes."

They sat in silence until he noticed her eyes on him. He sat up straighter and dusted his hands. "And I want to see him as soon as possible, so you need to get to work."

"Will you help me?"

Gonzo must have recognized the frailty in her question, as his features softened.

"I thought you'd never ask."

They worked through the afternoon, using boxes and totes they found in a spare bedroom to pack up the items Ren thought were most valuable to her or Kai's extended family. By dinnertime, they had used all the storage available at the house, and Gonzo volunteered to grab more boxes from a local store.

"It's quite a drive into town," Ren warned. "It'll take an hour."

"It's fine," he said. "The drive will give me a chance to call and ask Blane when his flight leaves."

"He's coming back?" she asked.

"Yeah. Well, he has to stop in Denver, but he should be back in a couple of days."

"That's great!" Ren said. "Have you thought about how you're going to ask him?"

A smile inched up on one side of his mouth. "I may fly to Denver. Like my dad used to say, it's burnin' a hole in my pocket."

"The ring?"

His mischievous grin spread across his face. "Sure. That's what I meant."

CHAPTER 24

She thought the knock at the door was Gonzo returning with the boxes. She ran to the door to help him with his load without checking the peephole. When she opened the door, Jonas took her in his arms.

His kiss was slow and sweet, and even though she intended to end their relationship, she returned his advances. Before she could think, they were on the kitchen floor, and it was half an hour later before they came up for breath.

He dressed slowly, as if he were waiting for her to attack him again. She thought about it, as she had no idea when she'd have sex again.

Jonas picked up the card. "Did you like them?" he asked, pointing to the roses.

Gonzo had been right. He had been trying to confirm her feelings for him. She wished she'd returned the card to the envelope before Jonas had arrived.

"They're lovely," she responded automatically.

"I don't know anything about flowers," he admitted. "My mother was the gardener in the family, and my brother was more like her than I was."

Ren could sense their conversation was shifting to a more negative topic, so she thought of another direction. "Are you hungry? Gonzo will be bringing food back for us soon. I can call and ask him to pick you up something, too."

Jonas shook his head. "I'm not going to eat until later. The water is warming up, and I'm going out on the boat with my brother."

Ren couldn't think of a response. It sounded like he was insinuating she should come along, but he already knew about her fear. Everyone knew.

He finally gave up on hinting. "I would like for you to come with us."

"No." Her response was swift and firm.

She had moved to a kitchen chair, and he joined her, scooting himself closely. "It would mean so much to me."

Ren was unmoved by his methods. It sounded narcissistic to her. "No."

"I know you've had a traumatic experience, but there's a reason you came up here. The lake is right outside. It's not a big monster you have to fight, but if you feel like you have to, I'll do it with you."

Jonas's words had hit their mark, and Ren's heart softened. She stared into his green eyes and saw sincerity. *Why had she been so quick to judge him?* What she had mistaken for narcissism was an attempt to help her.

Ren had thought about tackling her fear when she'd decided to stay at the lake house. She'd assumed she could approach it in baby steps, but she hadn't done more than close the window shade when a glint of the water caught her eye. *Could she be braver with Jonas by her side?*

Her resolve faltered. "I don't know. I—"

He took her hand and kissed her fingers. "I have life jackets, and if you get to the edge and decide you can't do it, I'll cover your eyes and carry you back here."

The image that was conjured up was funny to her, and she giggled. She could imagine Jonas stumbling through the sand in his cowboy boots with her in his arms.

He joined in her mirth. "You're so beautiful when you smile." He caressed her cheek, and she leaned into his hand. "Let me take away your fear."

Jonas was so kind and tender with her. She couldn't believe she'd considered running away from him. When she thought about how her actions would have compared to Collette's abandonment, it caused pain in her chest.

"I-I'll try."

He put gentle upward pressure on her hand, and she rose with him. "Grab your jacket, and we'll head down now."

Before I lose my nerve, she thought.

The lake whispered against the shore and tickled the edges of their shoes. Ren breathed in the earthy smell that spoke of the emerging vegetation. Soon, a dank scent would accompany it, but it wasn't enough to keep people from swimming or fishing.

"Can I leave you here while I get the boat?" Jonas whispered.

Ren nodded, but it was hard for her to let go of his hands. Jonas had been like an anchor, keeping her held to the safety of the land.

The minutes ticked by until she was certain that Jonas had forgotten her on the bank. An unfamiliar bird cried out, but when she looked for its source, Jonas hailed her from the water. He docked the boat, and when she didn't move to join him, he disembarked and stood at her side.

"Are you okay?" he asked. "This is a lot for today. Do you want to get on the boat tomorrow?"

She shook her head. She didn't trust her voice, as she feared it would be as shaky as her legs.

"Where's Riley?"

He shook his head as if that were the only explanation he could provide for his brother's absence.

He bent his head to assess her. "I want to help you, Ren, but I think you've had enough for today," he said, placing a hand on her back. "You're as white as a ghost."

His comment seemed fitting, as she was thinking about ghosts. The spirits in her mind were haunting her worse than the missing people who had disappeared around the lake, but the latter was a close second.

"I need to do it now," she told him.

Jonas's eyebrows drew together. "I don't think it's a good idea—"

She stopped his words with a glare. "You got me out here." There may have been more she wanted to say, but she couldn't bring the feelings to her lips.

He raised one of his hands to show he had given up and guided her to the boat. He let her lead them, and Ren was thankful for his comforting pats and words. Even though she had no idea what he was saying, his tone was comforting.

The boat rocked when she stepped onto it, but Ren imagined she was in an earthquake. Oddly, it was easier for her to imagine herself in a natural disaster than it was for her to believe she was on a mostly stable boat.

Memories of summers at the beach flooded back to her. Her father had taught her how to swim in long strokes, and her mother fileted the fish they'd caught during their morning boat ride out on the water.

Ren grabbed the seat closest to her. She had the presence of mind to see that she was on a pontoon boat and strapped herself into the belt at the base of her seat.

Her legs shook, and she desperately needed to urinate, but she was ready to go out on the lake. She gave Jonas an unconvincing smile.

"I'm going to start the boat now," he told her.

His movements were exaggerated, as he tried to let her know what he was doing far in advance of him doing it. Ren pretended to look around, but she focused on staying conscious and keeping the bile from traveling up her throat.

He rounded the corner, and the woods and houses fell away from view. Two buoys sat in the distance, bobbing from a boat's recent passing.

"I need to go back!" Ren shouted.

She realized her demand was sudden, but she couldn't process the idea of going out on the open water. The closeness of the shore had offered her some protection, and she wasn't ready to let it fall away.

The ride back to her dock was uneventful, but her bladder spasmed painfully as her nervousness intensified. As soon as the boat was close enough to the dock, Ren unbuckled herself and lunged for it. On stumbling legs, she ran to the shore, and as soon as her shoes touched the sand, she fell on it.

Contact with the earth brought tears to her eyes, but she didn't know she had been sobbing until Jonas picked her up. He carried her into the house without speaking.

Once inside, he continued upstairs and sat her on her bed. After he unhooked her life vest, he undressed her, but instead of taking her in his arms, he put her in a warm shower. She'd shivered as the water had warmed, and he'd covered her with a quilt. She thought about using it as her towel, but he took it with him as he left the room.

After the water had gone cold, Ren could get up and dress. She walked downstairs and noticed the warm smells of spice and sugar.

"Thank you for putting me in the shower," she said. "It was exactly what I needed."

Color blossomed on his cheeks. "After I saw the wet patch on your pants—"

He stopped speaking when her eyes widened. She hadn't known her bladder had let go, but she couldn't remember feeling the urgency to use the toilet after she'd collapsed on the shore. Humiliation churned her belly, and she covered her face.

Jonas took her hand and squeezed. "It's okay. You were so strong to go as far as you did today." He rested his forehead on hers.

Ren was thankful when he pulled away. She sat at the kitchen table and didn't look up until he put a plate of food under her nose.

"Cinnamon rolls," he announced, beaming at his creation.

The thick, buttery layers of dough spun into a circle, boasting gooey cream cheese icing at the center. It was too big to have come from a can and too large for Ren to finish.

"It's so good," she said every time she looked up. Jonas stared at her expectantly, and he seemed even more pleased when she repeated herself.

Midway through their meal, Ren jumped with a realization. "Where's Gonzo?"

Jonas finished chewing his bite before he answered. "I don't know. Didn't you say he was in town?"

Ren flew to the door, calling behind her. "Yeah. He should have been back by now, though."

Jonas held up Ren's cell phone when she got back to the table. "It didn't get damp."

Ren colored as she remembered why it would have been in danger of wetness. She whispered her appreciation.

She listened as the line beat back rings, but Gonzo didn't pick up. Voice mail was triggered, and she left a brief message.

Ren tried to keep her mind off her friend by playing a couple of card games with Jonas, but between each game, she drifted to the window, eyeing the empty parking space beside her car.

"You're really worried," Jonas observed.

Ren's fear for her friend's well-being caused her to lose patience with Jonas much faster than usual. She opened her mouth to let him know her feelings, but then she saw a piece of paper on the floor.

It may have been placed on the inside of the door, as the presence of tape indicated it had been pressed to a surface. Ren bent over and picked it up, noticing the curly script that belonged to Gonzo.

As she read the note, tears sprang to her eyes. Jonas stayed back, seemingly unsure of whether he should hold her or give her space.

She noticed him measuring her response and felt compelled to tell him what Gonzo had written. "When Gonzo came back, he saw us on the dock. He knew you were here to take care of me, so he felt free to go visit his boyfriend."

Ren left out the part in which Gonzo had torn her down for continuing her relationship with Jonas, and how he couldn't save her from her mistakes. In her mind, if she omitted those parts, then she didn't have to face what it spoke about her character.

After she relayed the parts of the letter she wanted to share with Jonas, Ren bolted upstairs. Gonzo had left no sign of his presence. He'd even made the bed.

"He didn't tell me goodbye," she spoke aloud.

Jonas put his hands on her shoulders, squeezing them once. "He's a grown man. He went after someone he loved." He turned Ren around to face him. "I can understand that."

She hoped he wasn't hinting that he loved her, but Ren was too upset about her friend's sudden departure to ask him about it. Instead, she let him encircle her in his arms.

Jonas lowered his head, placing a kiss on the tip of her nose. "Do you want to finish eating or go to bed?"

Ren couldn't pull herself away from his tender embrace. "I couldn't eat another bite, but I need to clean up."

Sensing her reluctance to leave him, Jonas led her to the bedroom. "We can take care of it tomorrow."

Chapter 25

en thought she'd wake in a tangle of arms and legs, but Jonas was gone.

She sat up in the bed and noticed the slant of the sun through the windows. The birds chirped merrily outside. A nest was close to her window. She called out for Jonas, but she didn't expect an answer.

Feet pounded up the steps. When he appeared in her room, she noticed he had on a fresh shirt and jeans.

"Did you change?"

He glanced at his reflection in the mirror, walking toward the dresser on which it rested as he fussed over the part in his hair. "I ran home to take a shower and change."

He climbed into bed with her, kicking off his shoes, and pulling her body to him. She did her best not to show irritation, but the material of his shirt was bristly against her skin. He noticed her moving away as they kissed.

"Is something wrong?"

Ren decided to be honest, and she explained her sensitivity to his shirt's fabric.

"I know how to take care of that." He smiled, wriggling out of his shirt and tossing it onto the floor along with the rest of his clothes.

She woke alone again, but the smell of food let her know Jonas's location.

She slid out of bed, dressed quickly, and joined him in the kitchen. "Something smells delicious."

"It's chicken and dumplings," he announced.

He had taken another shower and put on a different shirt. It seemed more cottony and comfortable than the ones he'd worn in the past.

Ren put her arms around his neck and stared up at him. "You didn't have to change your shirt."

He seemed puzzled, but then he looked down at his clothes as if noticing them for the first time. "I thought it'd be more comfortable."

They ate in comfortable silence. Ren was glad Jonas was a good cook, as she didn't like to make food. Too much went into preparing it, so she usually fixed a box dinner or ordered out.

Ren pointed to the late morning sun. "You know, I find it funny that we're eating dumplings for breakfast, and we had cinnamon rolls for dinner."

Jonas ran a hand through his slicked-back hair. "My brother and I lived with really strict parents, so when they died, we decided to do things the way we wanted."

"Sounds interesting," Ren said through a mouthful of dumplings.

"Like that." Jonas pointed his spoon at her mouth. "We would have been sent to the hole for the rest of the day if we had talked with food in our mouths."

Heat rose from Ren's chest, and she hurried to finish her bite. "I'm sorry."

Jonas shook his head. "Don't be." He took a small bite and spoke through it. "We don't live by their rules anymore."

Something in his story had bothered Ren. "What was *the hole*?"

"It was our basement."

"Why did they put you in the basement?" Ren had never raised a child, but she was certain it was an uncommon punishment.

Jonas continued to eat without looking at her. "It was our mother. She knew we were afraid of the dark, so she'd leave us down there and take the bulb from the light."

"That's awful," Ren said before she could stop herself.

Jonas shrugged. "There was a small window on the east side, so we stayed under it until the sun went down."

"She left you there overnight?"

"Sometimes."

Ren put down her spoon, unsettled. "Why didn't your father intervene?"

Another shrug. "He worked, and he left her in charge of us. When he got home, he went to the same easy chair and stayed in it until Mother woke him up for work the next day."

"He even slept there?"

Jonas nodded and twirled the spoon around his bowl. "He said he liked the view of the lake from there."

"Didn't he hear you guys in the basement? Your house has a similar construction as this one, and I heard that animal—"

"He heard us once."

Ren wondered if she should say more. Jonas beat her to it.

"She'd pushed Riley a little too hard down the stairs, and he hurt his arm. He cried and cried, but I couldn't do anything but scream for her to take him to the hospital."

He took a shuddering breath. "Just before my dad got home, she came down the stairs and duct-taped our mouths shut."

Ren gasped. "You poor boys!"

He pushed his bowl to the end of his placemat. "Yeah. She was pretty hard on us."

"Did your brother ever get to the hospital?"

He nodded. "We waited until we knew she was in bed, and we felt our way up the stairs. We beat the door until our knuckles were bloody, and we finally woke up our dad. He peeled the tape off our mouths and pulled us into his truck. Mother ran outside, but he pushed her into the mud and screamed at her."

He sipped his water. "Riley was okay. He got a bright pink cast and had all the nurses sign it before he left." He chuckled. "He was always a Casanova, even at nine."

Ren's eyes widened. "You were only nine?"

He traced the pattern on the placemat, avoiding her eyes. "Yeah. She couldn't do as much to us as we got older."

Ren's hand went to her mouth. "Your father didn't leave her after that?"

"He didn't know how to raise children, and she fed him some pack of lies about how we'd misbehaved."

Ren couldn't imagine any scenario that justified that type of punishment. "I'm so sorry, Jonas."

He looked up at her. "It's okay." He put on a faux smile that reminded her of some of the ones she'd worn in the past. "That's why we don't play by her rules anymore."

Before she could offer more consolation, he popped out of his chair and reached out to her. "Are you ready to go somewhere?"

"Where?" Ren took his hand and allowed him to help her stand.

"Anywhere."

His tone suggested the urgency with which he needed to leave, and after hearing his sad story, Ren was more than happy to accommodate him.

Ren and Jonas ended up driving for part of the afternoon and spending the evening at a restaurant that bordered the lake. Unlike the weighty topic they'd discussed earlier, their conversations were light.

"It sounds like you had a great time!" Ren laughed, catching her lover's smile as he described a drunken night out on the lake when he and his brother were teenagers.

"It was pretty fun," he agreed, the subtle lines around his eyes creasing. "Until my brother popped me into the lake with an oar."

Ren joined his merriment, but her own fear of water prompted her next question. "But you were drinking. Couldn't you have drowned?"

He took a long pull off his third beer. "Never. I'm a strong swimmer, and my brother is, too. He would have pulled me out."

He threw up a finger, indicating that he had to excuse himself.

While he was gone, Ren took in the view. The lake lapped lazily against the sand, looking less foreboding now that she had matched her date beer for beer.

The server stopped at the table and looked her over. Her worried eyes pleaded with her over a thin nose and pale lips.

"I need to tell you something," she said, casting worried looks in the direction Jonas had gone. "You need to get away from him."

"What?" Ren straightened in her chair.

The woman leaned over the table, her loose shirt falling danger-ously close to the cup of barbecue sauce Jonas hadn't finished. "I can help you. Just tell him you have to go to the bathroom, and I'll call a driver for you."

Ren realized her mouth was open. "Why?"

"Don't you know about them?" Her eyes widened. "I thought everyone around here knew about what happened."

Ren could only stare at her. She must have shaken her head, as the woman leaned closer, darting a look at the bathrooms where the door to the men's room was opening.

The server began clearing the table, but she managed to whisper, "He and his brother killed their mother."

CHAPTER 26

en was quiet for the rest of the evening. When Jonas mentioned it, she claimed she had a headache.

He stayed with her, throwing his arm over her as he slept. Ren lay awake for the longest time, wondering how she could ask him about his mother's death. She decided she would look up the obituary.

Once she'd figured out her next step, Ren thought sleep would find her easily, but the moon slid shadows across the walls for hours before she concluded that her brain wanted her to take immediate action. She moved out from under Jonas's arm and noted the gentle puffs of air that still came from him. She hoped he'd stay asleep.

She grabbed her laptop off the dresser where she usually kept it and crept downstairs. She thought every creek would give her away, but the rest of the house remained motionless.

The light from her laptop hurt her eyes, so she turned down the brightness and jumped on the internet. Cell service was sometimes spotty around the lake, but the Wi-Fi service always worked inside the house.

Jonas had mentioned that his mother's name was Mary, so she searched for the obituary of a Mary with his surname. Hundreds of results popped up, but when she narrowed her search, it listed none of the women in the area.

She sat back and sighed, rubbing her tired eyes. She felt the faintest touch on her shoulder, and she whipped around.

Jonas had leaned against the back of the couch, squatting until he was level with her range of sight. "What has you up so late?" He looked at the waning night. "Or early?"

Ren closed her laptop with a snap. "I'm just researching a character."

"Someone with my mother's name?"

She was busted. It was best to come clean.

"I was a little upset by what you told me about her earlier."

His jaw clenched as he stared at her. Ren was growing uncomfortable under his almost expressionless gaze.

"What more do you want to know?" he asked. "She was a witch, and she's burning in—"

"I'm so sorry." Ren put her hand on his face, hoping to soften his features with her touch. "I should have left it alone."

He nodded once, accepting her apology, but giving her nothing more. She followed him upstairs, hanging her head as she watched his heels.

He stopped at the base of the steps. "Could you get me a glass of water?"

By the time Ren filled the glass and made it back to the room, Jonas was asleep. She put the water on the nightstand beside him and crawled into bed.

As she was about to doze off, she heard a scream. She jolted upright, waking Jonas.

"What was that?"

Jonas rubbed his eyes. "I didn't hear anything, but I'll check it out if you want me to."

"I have a gun in the top drawer of the dresser," she told him.

He stopped rubbing his eyes. "Is it loaded?"

She shook her head before she realized he couldn't see her. "No. I don't even know if there are bullets for it in the house. It was—" She stopped herself before she said her husband's name. "It's not really mine."

Jonas disentangled himself from the bedsheets and tiptoed out of the room. She heard him move across the house, opening the closet and utility doors. By the time he made it to the basement, she was behind him.

He turned the knob as he whispered fiercely. "Go back upstairs!"

"But what if you get attacked?" she whispered back.

He stopped and stared at her. "Then you'll get attacked, too."

Ren understood his logic, but she opted to stay in the living room, near the door, until she heard his feet pad up the steps. He found her easily and rested an arm on her shoulder.

"I don't know what you heard, but everything is fine. It wasn't anything in the house."

"I was dozing," she admitted. "I could have dreamed it."

He patted her shoulder. "That seems like a good explanation."

They went back to bed, and after her late-night anxieties had abated, Ren slept well into the afternoon. She woke refreshed, but she had a nagging feeling she'd missed something important. She couldn't shake it. It was like the feeling was attached to a line with a hook that was lodged in her brain. Every time she tried to think of something else, it would reel her back.

The more she thought about it, the more she believed it had something to do with the sound she'd heard. Her tired mind could have conjured up a scream, but the voice had sounded so real. She didn't know if it had been masculine or feminine, but the sound haunted her for days.

Could someone have been in her house calling for her to help?

CHAPTER 27

R en didn't like to think about the accident or the year preceding her husband's death. It was a dark time, with only a few rays of sun penetrating the gloom.

Looking back, there were things she noticed, but she stayed blind. There were conversations she heard, but she let them fall on deaf ears, and there were times she could have spoken up, but she remained silent.

She believed she could have saved her husband, but she let him go. She may not have taken his life, but her actions, or inactions, led to his death.

The doctors told her he had intracranial hypertension.

Ren got on her hands and knees and prayed as her family surrounded her. She begged and pleaded with a creator she had never really known, promising to do anything He wanted in exchange for Kai's life.

She drank countless cups of coffee to stay awake, never allowing herself more than a doze. If she noticed sleep taking over, she'd jump up and walk around, sometimes with a fierceness that surprised the ones around her.

She was convinced she was the reason her husband was in the hospital. If she had asked him to wait to celebrate their anniversary until the weekend, he would have listened. If she would have been better at seducing him, Kai would have gotten a hotel in Asheville. If she wouldn't have pestered him so much, he wouldn't have used so much of his energy fighting with her.

Ren could feel the eyes of the hospital staff on her. They knew she was guilty. She knew they were condemning her for Kai's condition.

Ren's prayers were answered, even though she never thought of them again or made good on her promises. When they finally allowed her to see him, Kai looked too vulnerable for her to touch him. The nurse encouraged her to speak, but Ren felt like she was delivering a soliloquy instead of speaking to her husband.

A doctor visited the room after days that had gone by in a blur. He announced her husband had a hypoxic brain injury, and it was unclear if he'd recover.

"In fact, I doubt he will ever fully recover," he'd told her. "He was underwater too long without oxygen."

When Kai woke up and recognized her, Ren was overjoyed. He was going to be one of the patients who defied their prognoses.

Kai tried to live up to her expectations. He attended every physical therapy and mental evaluation. Ren found out later that his cognition had declined, but when he'd reported positively about his sessions, Ren had accepted his words. She wanted things to go back to normal. If Kai recovered and lived the same as he had before the accident, then Ren believed it would absolve her of the guilt she felt.

After three months, he went back to work. He claimed his leave had taken a large chunk out of their finances, but Ren suspected he needed to get out of the house. She didn't talk him out of it, as a return to his schedule was a step in the right direction.

Kai won his first two cases, but his third case revealed something Ren had dreaded. During the wrap-up, he forgot the name of the case he was referencing. He stood with a vague look on his face, stretching to grab the name of a case that thousands of his fellow attorneys had easily referenced.

His partner mentioned a vacation, but Kai refused to take a step back so soon after his return to the firm. He didn't tell Ren, opting instead to keep her in the dark. Ren obliged until Christmas.

The holiday fell after a weekend, so Ren didn't set her clock. It baffled her when Kai jumped out of bed, cursing. She asked him what was wrong.

"The alarm didn't go off!"

She picked up the alarm and realized the day. "I didn't set it. It's—"

"You didn't set it?" He stopped to stare her down. The early morning light wasn't enough to shine on the darkness around his eyes.

"It's Christmas." Her voice trembled.

"What? It's not—"

Ren pulled the blanket higher, as if it would protect her from his anger. "Please, Kai. Go check the calendar."

Since he'd started working, Kai had gotten into the habit of drawing a line through the day right before he went to bed. Sensing it was for a good reason, Ren had crossed dates off the calendar when he had fallen asleep before making his mark.

Kai huffed and strode downstairs. As he checked her claim, Ren hurried and dressed. There was something about being naked as he yelled at her that made her feel more vulnerable.

He came back into the room as she was zipping up her jeans. He was much quieter than he had been when he'd stormed out of the room.

"You're right. It's—"

He stopped speaking when Ren jumped. She turned around quickly, and his eyes narrowed.

"What's wrong with you?"

Ren pasted on a smile. "Everything's fine."

He eyed her for another beat before he apologized for yelling at her. She soaked in his apology and set to work on their breakfast.

After they'd eaten, Ren prepared to visit her family. She didn't hear her husband getting ready, and he seemed surprised when she mentioned it was time to go.

Kai exaggerated a yawn. "I'm still really tired. Can you go without me?"

The keys dangled in Ren's hand. "No, Kai. I will not go to a family function without you. We've gone every year, and my mother is counting on you to carve the ham."

He sighed and bounced out of his leather chair. "Fine."

After the accident, anytime they went anywhere, Ren drove. They never discussed the change. Kai simply popped into the passenger seat of her mid-sized luxury car.

At her parent's house, hugs were exchanged, and she helped her mother in the kitchen. When she questioned Ren about their lateness, Ren responded she'd overslept.

Kai carved the ham, and they shared a large meal. Too full to leave the table afterward, they opted to drink coffee and talk.

"What did Kai get you this year?" her mother asked. "I love hearing about his gifts."

In the years preceding the accident, Kai had lavished Ren with expensive gifts from cars to jewelry. This Christmas had been different. He had forgotten about the holiday, so he hadn't picked out anything for her.

Ren squirmed in her seat under her mother's expectant gaze. She hung her head as Kai intervened.

"She hasn't gotten it yet."

Thankfully, he knew the right words to say to convince her parents he had a nice surprise planned for her. Ren understood it was an act to save his face as well as her pride, but she didn't mind.

Ren had gotten a knife for her father and Blue Ridge Pottery for her mother. Her parents had stood over them beaming as Kai and Ren unwrapped two tickets for a train ride.

"It's in North Carolina," her father had explained. "You may want to wait until they finish their Polar Express rides."

Her mother piped up. "The two of you could go next fall when the leaves change. The tickets are good for a year."

Before they left, Ren's father pulled her into the hallway. Her mother was busy loading Kai down with leftovers while she told him about the recent drama at her book club.

"Is Kai okay?" her father asked, his bushy eyebrows drawing together.

Ren responded automatically. "Yeah. Why?"

He stared at the floor and grabbed his chin, stroking the stubble that always appeared in the evening. "He didn't recognize the teams."

Ren was puzzled. "What do you mean?"

"We were watching the football game, and Green Bay scored a touchdown. I looked over to rib him about his team, but he just sat there. When I said something to him about it, he acted like it was no big deal. Wasn't he born in Wisconsin?"

Kai had Brett Farve's autographed football in his office and a Packer's jersey in a glass case.

"I think he has had some things on his mind," she explained quickly. "He didn't mean to ruin the game for you."

Her father's features went from concerned to apologetic. "No, honey, he didn't ruin the game. I was just worried that it might have something to do with the accident."

"Not at all," she assured him. "He's been back at work for the past five months, and he's doing well."

Part of her knew it was a lie. The other part urged her to continue with her optimism.

Kai stepped to the edge of the hallway, and her mother locked eyes with her father, throwing up her hands. He must have shared the topic he wanted to discuss with her mother before he'd led Ren away.

Either their smiles were too wide, or their position in the hallway gave away the seriousness of their discussion, as Kai's smile faltered. "What's up?"

Ren continued her faux smile. "I was just telling Dad how much we'll enjoy the tickets he gave us."

Kai's expression changed. "Are you sure you weren't sharing something more with him?"

His tone was playful, and it confused Ren. "No." She drew out the vowel.

Her mother gasped and brought her hands to her face. "Are you pregnant?"

Ren drew in a breath to voice her answer and choked. "No," she coughed out.

Kai put a hand on her mother's shoulder as she deflated. "That may not be for long." He waggled his eyebrows at Ren.

Her father cringed. "I don't care if it's for a baby. Talking about my daughter's sex life is still a taboo subject for me." He ducked out of the hallway after hugging Ren. "You two have a good night."

"We will, Dad," Kai teased, poking at his ribs as he tried to slide past him.

Ren's father almost ran into the next room, holding his hands over his ears. "La, la, la."

Ren closed her mouth with a pop. She and Kai had decided they would remain childless before they got married. *Why was Kai filling her mother's head with false hope?*

"Are you serious?" Her mother's cheeks blossomed with color. "I could be a grandmother this time next year?"

He nodded his head. They hugged while Ren tried to decide on something to say.

"I think we should talk about this."

Her mother looked from Kai to her. "I thought you two had already discussed it."

"I was going to talk to her about it later," Kai told her without looking at Ren. "But I'm sure she'll agree. Every woman wants a baby."

Ren felt anger rise from her chest. "Not *every* woman."

Kai's smile faded, and her mother cleared her throat. Ren kissed her mother's cheek. "Thank you for the lovely holiday, Mom."

Kai echoed her sentiments, following her out the door. His footsteps pounded the sidewalk and then crunched the ice behind her.

"Give me the keys."

"No," Ren said simply. "It's my car."

"I paid for it," he countered. "It's actually *my* car."

Ren froze. Kai had never separated their possessions, but then she remembered she had claimed personal ownership over it.

She handed him the keys.

It had been a long time since she'd ridden in the passenger seat. She adjusted her settings, making the temperature on her side of the car much warmer than Kai preferred.

Kai waited until they got on the road before he spoke again. "What did you think you were doing back there?"

She glared at him. "I told you before we got married. I don't want children."

He made short glances at her as he drove. "Why? Because you're so selfish?"

"Selfish?" Ren echoed.

Kai mimicked her voice. "I don't want to be held back by kids. Can you imagine having to leave work early because your child was sick?"

Ren colored and looked away. "I'm still not ready."

His grip on the steering wheel tightened. "Obviously. I thought you'd grown a little over the past four years, but you're still the same selfish girl who slept with me on the second date."

Ren looked up. "Are you serious? We're married now, and I felt a connection to you. I haven't been with that many people."

"Could've fooled me," he shot back.

Ren wanted to say something to wound him, but everything she thought of was too deep. She couldn't say anything about the accident and risk him voicing the blame she knew he directed at her.

"I don't want your baby."

He was quiet, and that wasn't good. Usually, he would rant at her until their argument fizzled out, but his silence was more distressing.

Ren noticed the speedometer moving up. It was gradual at first, but then trees whipped past her.

"Stop it, Kai. You'll wreck us."

He turned his blazing eyes on her. "You mean like I did last spring?"

Ren looked out her window, hoping her silence would make him slow down. Instead, he pushed his foot down harder.

Ren was thankful they were on the interstate. Any other road would have had more cars.

They passed a sixteen-wheeler so fast that Ren couldn't read the advertisement on the side. When she looked back at Kai, he was hardly looking at the road, an evil grin on his face.

She made her voice as calm as possible. "Stop it. You're scaring me."

"Really?" He pressed on the accelerator so hard he was almost standing on it. "I wonder what that feels like."

"Stop it, Kai."

He kept going as if she hadn't spoken. "I wonder what it would be like to be left underwater while your wife makes a speedy getaway."

"You weren't even conscious," she shot back. "I couldn't get out on my own. Someone pulled me out."

"Your boyfriend?" his eyebrows shot up. "Maybe you'll have *his* baby."

Ren's anger was threatening to erupt, but she tried to establish some peace. "He's not my boyfriend, and I don't want to have anyone's baby. Please stop the car."

Kai spat at her. "I hate you."

Ren didn't have time to be shocked by the saliva dangling from her hair. A bright red car flashed across her vision, and Kai swerved, narrowly missing it.

The close call seemed to be enough, as he let off on the accelerator and pulled to the shoulder of the road. He buried his face in his hands and cried.

"I'm so sorry," he repeated until Ren held him and rocked.

She drove them the rest of the way home. When they walked into the house, he picked her up and carried her to their bedroom.

He said all the words she was used to hearing and made promises she didn't know if he could keep. Ren was so glad to feel his love and attention that she fell under his spell.

Before they made love, he looked at her with tears still dotting his dark lashes. "Please. Just this once. Don't make me use protection."

Ren only stared at him. He took her silence as acceptance.

She never expected it would only take one time.

CHAPTER 28

"It was our first summer together," Jonas explained, holding a picture of Kai and him.

Other than leaving briefly when she slept, Jonas had been at the lake house for a week. Secretly, Ren wished he'd stay at the house he shared with his brother, but Jonas showed no signs of going back to their previous arrangement.

"We were eight," he went on. He pointed, and Ren followed his finger to the lake. "We were on that dock, completely soaked after we went swimming in the water hole."

Ren settled back on the couch. "Where's that?"

Apparently, Ren had moved too far away from him when she leaned back, and he placed his arm around her. "It's just past my house. I could take you there sometime."

He chatted about the uncertain depth of the water, and Ren's mind drifted. Any other woman would be thrilled to have such an attentive boyfriend, but she was tired of his affection. She wanted to go home and leave the lake house behind.

She liked Jonas, and he was good to her, but she associated him with her ex-husband. The more Ren thought about her situation, the more she believed she should sell both houses and start a new chapter in her life.

Jonas stopped speaking, and it took a beat before Ren answered him. "Yeah. I think I can go to the water hole. You don't expect me to swim there, right?"

He glanced away. "I'd hoped we could swim, but it's okay if you aren't ready."

They started drinking at lunch and were already on their second bottle of wine. The alcohol empowered her, and she jumped up.

"I'll get my swimsuit."

Ren didn't think about where they were going. She stayed in the moment, attempting to free her mind of any anxieties.

Her dulled senses helped her enjoy the scenery around the lake in a way she hadn't since Kai drove them into the water. She noticed budding trees and flowers and the bubbles the fish made as they swam close to the surface.

Jonas walked past his house, throwing worried looks at the windows. He almost seemed afraid of his brother, but Ren couldn't imagine why. It seemed they had bonded over the traumatic events of their youth, so it should have brought them closer in their adulthood.

They chose to live together, Ren thought. Adult men usually didn't do that unless they had a good relationship.

Their destination was much closer than Ren realized. The lake ended in almost a cul-de-sac, and an area to the side of Jonas's house revealed a cave and water hole.

The cave was so small that Ren could see the back of it from where she stood, and the surrounding vegetation was well-maintained. The water from the lake filtered into the hole, but if a boat casually passed by, the occupants would miss the area.

There was something serene in the atmosphere. It was almost like a woodland oasis, where they could see the world around them while tucked away from prying eyes.

Jonas took her in his arms. "Thank you for coming here with me." Ren was still busy absorbing the sights and sounds around her when he added, "I love you."

Ren's automatic response was to return the sentiment, but she held her tongue. It was too soon for Jonas to profess his love, and she wasn't going to encourage him by going along with it.

Her silence stretched on until Jonas laughed nervously. "You don't have to say it back. I know it's probably hard for you to love anyone after what happened."

How had he known what had happened? It hadn't been covered. It wasn't circulated on the news either.

"I know I said I wanted to take things slowly, but I fell so hard for you." He cupped her cheek in his palm. "When you look at me, I can see our future."

Once Kai had spoken similar words to her, and before the accident, she'd believed him. Even though Jonas had good intentions, she couldn't bring herself to embrace him.

"I need some time."

He blinked several times and took a step away. "Of course. Let me know how much time you need."

Ren was a little shocked when he stood still, waiting for her answer. She borrowed Gonzo's way of injecting humor into uncomfortable situations.

"Let me get through this first." She motioned to the water.

Jonas smiled good-naturedly. "Lead the way."

When Ren took off her shirt and put on her bathing suit, he put a hand on her arm. "We don't need suits here."

Jonas stripped his clothes and jumped into the water, coming up quickly and shouting from the temperature.

"We may not want to do this today. The water is freezing!" He popped out and dressed quickly.

Ren stood holding her bathing suit top in one hand and her shirt in the other. "Shouldn't I try it?"

The question was more for herself than for him, but Jonas answered her. "It's a real shock when you hit the water. I wouldn't do it."

"But what if this is my chance to break my fear?"

Jonas touched his frigid fingers to her arm. "I wouldn't want you to miss out on an opportunity just because of a little cold water."

Ren dropped her clothes and shimmied out of her jeans. She ran to the water, but at the edge she stopped, staring at the murky brown depths.

She didn't know how long she stood there before she felt Jonas pull her shirt over her head. "I think that's enough." His voice was gentle but firm. "Thank you for coming with me."

She let him guide her back to the house. Time seemed to skip, and before she could fully register a change, she was in her living room with a blanket wrapped around her.

Smells of sweet chili floated to her, and she closed her eyes. She should have joined him, offering to make cornbread to accompany it, but she couldn't bring herself to lift from her seat.

Jonas brought her food on a tray with old cartoon characters. She didn't know if it had been the only one in the house, but she would have felt more comfortable eating at the table. It was odd to have multicolored bears stare at her as she ate, but it was even more awkward to have the tray over her lap with her new lover beside her.

She put one of her hands on the couch, and Jonas covered it with his own. "I have to stay at my house tonight. Will you be okay?"

Finally, she thought, *a night to myself!*

Ren kept her expression neutral. "I'll be fine." She didn't trust herself to say more, as she was afraid she'd reveal her excitement.

He squeezed her hand. "I'll check on you in the morning. I made the chili in the electric pot, and I left it on. You can have more if you get hungry."

Ren felt like a guest in her own home. She was glad for the option, but she was perfectly capable of making her own food.

When Jonas left, it was all she could do to keep herself from jumping with joy. She walked around the house, staring at the boxes she'd packed, and wondered if she should rent a storage building for them. Excited by the prospect of getting something done, Ren loaded as many boxes as she could into her car and left.

The nearest city was Johnson City, and it took her over an hour to get there. The process for securing a storage building was pretty simple, but the manager asked her some strange questions. He said bodies had been recently discovered in a storage building in Erwin, so he was more cautious about his renters.

The building he gave her was the size of a small room. Once Ren unloaded her car, the boxes filled about a sixteenth of the space.

She picked up some ice cream and went back to the lake. She thought about stopping at her house, but she was tired.

Ren chose a movie and ate half the carton of ice cream. When she placed her bowl in the sink, she noticed Jonas had left a bottle of wine in the refrigerator for her. She poured a glass and took the bottle upstairs with her.

She dialed Gonzo's number, and it rang until voicemail picked it up. She left a message, but she couldn't remember what she'd said after she hung up. She tried to send a text, but she erased half of the words and gave up.

She missed her friend so much. She'd trade a thousand men like Jonas to have her friend with her. If she could go back in time, she would have left Jonas standing at the door, knocking until his knuckles bled.

The curser on her laptop blinked until her second glass of wine, and then she wrote through a third. She was amazed by the words that flew onto the screen, but she couldn't focus on the thoughts behind them.

She crawled into bed and tried to wrap herself in happy memories. Her thoughts flitted from her happy childhood to her first experiences with Kai, landing on the most traumatic event in her life. She fell asleep with the past pulling her down into a place her mind rarely let her go.

Chapter 29

Kai started going to the lake house every weekend. At first, it was a relief to be free of the burden of his broodiness, but after a month, Ren felt lonely.

She went to spring festivals and ate all the junk food she could find, from funnel cakes to cotton candy. She saw some of Kai's friends while she was out, and they'd ask about him. She told them he was swimming and diving at the lake, and they'd nod and excuse themselves politely when they realized she wasn't as vibrant in a conversation as her spouse.

Even though it hadn't improved Ren's social skills, pregnancy had given her more confidence, and she had gone to more shops. She was excited about the life growing inside her and she wanted him or her to have boutique clothes and a themed nursery.

She had been upset when she'd learned about her pregnancy, denying the child she conceived on a night she wanted to forget. After a couple of weeks, though, she imagined her life with a baby, and her feelings softened.

Even though she was a grown woman with a husband, Ren was nervous about sharing her pregnancy. She saw men give up their seats on the bus for pregnant women, and she didn't want to be obligated to accept their goodwill. Everyone in her family would fly into preparations for a baby shower, too, and Ren wasn't ready for it. She was scared, but not because she was a new mother.

Ren had spotted. She'd thought she'd had a period until it ended four days too soon and she felt nauseated. She made an appointment, and her gynecologist ordered a blood test. They confirmed her pregnancy by phone and urged her to come back in three days for another test. Her doctor explained that her HcG levels continued to rise, so she had probably experienced implantation bleeding.

Ren was still nervous about revealing her condition to Kai, so she waited. After another week, she spotted again. This time, she was convinced she was having a miscarriage, and her doctor ordered an ultrasound. The wand they inserted revealed a growing embryo with a rapid heartbeat, and no problems were detected.

Still, Ren had kept her condition a secret from her husband until she was almost twelve weeks pregnant, convincing herself that the blood would reappear once she shared the news. If it weren't for the fried hamburger meat, she wouldn't have been discovered.

Kai made most of his meals, citing Ren's inability to cook. In reality, the pair had different tastes, with Kai preferring more Asian dishes and Ren enjoying American and Italian meals.

Kai had arrived home from work in a good mood. He'd made some progress with a divorce case, and he kept his positivity flowing by cooking a meal Ren liked.

The smell of baked ziti filled the house, pushing its delicious scent toward her from all directions. She drifted into the kitchen as Kai placed the last plate on the table. He poured wine into her glass, and Ren allowed him to help her into her chair.

After the first bite, Ren's stomach soured. She tried to listen attentively as her husband described his day, but every time she bit down on her food, she felt the need to spit it out. The ziti didn't smell right, and she was convinced the meat had gone beyond its recommended usage date. When she asked Kai about it, he'd exploded.

"Why do you have to ruin everything I do for you?" He stared at her with his eyes darting like he was reading her face. "You do it on purpose, don't you?"

Ren's temper, which she usually held in check, boiled. "All I do is try to make you happy!"

Shocked by her snappy reply, it took a minute for Kai to respond. "You could have fooled me." He motioned in the air. "Look at this place. You don't clean all day, and when I get home, I have to cook for both of us."

Ren tossed her fork onto her plate. "You don't have to cook for me. I'd rather not eat spoiled meat."

Kai picked up her plate, and she thought he was going to throw it into the sink, but he dumped the contents into her lap. He sneered down at her, waiting for her response.

Ren stood up. She was half a foot shorter than Kai, but she held his eyes.

The slap she gave him echoed off the walls. His hand went automatically to his cheek, but instead of backing down, he grabbed her arms.

Ren didn't know what would have happened next. Her mind flew to her unborn child and her need to protect her baby.

"I'm pregnant," she blurted.

Kai's eyes were dark with fury, and his jaw clenched. Her news almost instantly smoothed the landscape of his face.

"What?"

She didn't dare move, but she willed herself to keep talking. Whatever violence he was going to do had been paused.

"I'm going to have a baby. I'm due in the middle of September."

Kai's mouth twitched. It wasn't a happy smile, and, to her, it seemed self-satisfied.

"It was on Christmas, wasn't it?"

She nodded once. She looked down at his hands, and he loosened his grip.

"That's wonderful news," he went on as if he hadn't been ready to hurt her. "I have a few cases that will go to court around that time, but I'll see if I can move them around."

Now that Ren had cooled his temper, she wasn't going to let the hostility of his actions go unnoticed. "What's wrong with you? Why were you about to hit me?"

He chuckled, and Ren bristled. "You know I never would have hurt you." He released her. "You're the one who hurt me."

Ren thought about it. She had struck her husband.

They'd had a lot of arguments, but they usually walked away from each other before it became too heated. Since the accident, Kai had been more combative, but he hadn't hit her. Maybe she was to blame for striking him.

"I'm sorry."

He placed a hand on her cheek. "I know you didn't mean it. Your hormones must be everywhere right now."

She wasn't happy with his condescending tone. She looked down at the ziti that had made a stain on her pink and white outfit.

She thought Kai was going to apologize to her for dumping her meal onto her lap, but he glossed over it. "I bet those same hormones are responsible for your reaction to the meal I made for you."

He smiled magnanimously. "I can make something else for you while you clean up." He picked up her wineglass, swirling its contents. "This certainly isn't for you tonight."

Ren hadn't touched wine in weeks, opting to throw it down the sink after her meals. She'd been lucky her husband had been self-absorbed, and he hadn't noticed her wineglass as he had drained the bottle.

Ren had taken a shower and put on a soft nightgown that revealed a small baby bump. Ren thought she looked pregnant, but to most people, her growing belly would have seemed like the result of overindulgence at dinner.

Kai welcomed her with crackers and ginger ale. "I downloaded a pregnancy app, and it mentioned this" —he motioned to the food— "was good for you."

She sat down on the couch, and he put the snack on the end table beside her. He pulled her feet into his lap and massaged them.

She chose the movie they watched while he flicked through his phone. "How many weeks are you?"

"Eleven," Ren answered hesitantly.

He shot her a disapproving glance. "You should have told me. Early prenatal care is critical."

"I've been going to the doctor," Ren told him. "I had a little bleeding, and—"

His grip on her foot tightened until she lost her breath. He let go after a few seconds, but his disapproval was clear.

"How many people knew before me?"

She opened her mouth to answer and paused. His fingers had tightened around her foot again. It wasn't enough to cause discomfort, but she knew he could hurt her easily if her answer displeased him.

"Just the doctor and the nurse."

His eyebrow twitched. "Not even your mother."

Ren shook her head vigorously.

"That's good. We can start telling people—"

Ren put a hand on his arm. "Can we wait? I want us to enjoy the pregnancy for a little while before we let everyone else know."

He measured her, seeming to look for an alternate reason for her request. He nodded as if his consent was all she'd needed.

They watched the movie, but neither one of them seemed to enjoy it. Ren assumed Kai was as lost in his thoughts as her, but she didn't want to question him and disrupt the peace.

"I need to stay home more," he said as the credits rolled. "I won't go to the lake house as much."

Ren had gotten used to her weekends alone. Even though she had been lonely occasionally, she couldn't imagine sharing all her time with the man her husband had become.

"Oh, you don't have to do that," she objected. "You deserve to have time to reset after your hard week and clear your head."

He thought about it. "You're probably right. I want to do some diving, and spring and summer are the perfect time to explore more of the lake."

"I'll stay home on the weekends after the baby's born," he told her, patting her belly. "We'll be a happy family."

Ren let a smile inch across her lips, but she kept her true feelings to herself. Kai could make plans for their future, but she had no intention of staying with him or of keeping their baby.

CHAPTER 30

S he woke when the bed moved.

At first, she thought she'd imagined it, but the slight movement of her blanket continued until an arm encircled her. A kiss on her shoulder awakened her desire. She wished she could turn him away, but she grabbed for a condom in the drawer next to her.

Liquid seeped into her hands, and she opened her eyes, checking the package. "There's a hole in this one. Did you bring another one?"

Jonas rose in the dark and walked over to his discarded jeans. In the low light, Ren watched him whip out his wallet, removing a condom from the inside fold.

Jonas was rougher with her than usual, but he was still attentive to her needs. Afterward, she drifted off to sleep, and when she woke, he was gone, making her wonder if he had been there at all.

Jonas didn't wander back into the house until after three o'clock, giving her plenty of time to shower and review her drunken evening. Ren wasn't surprised by the mix of words and letters she had sent to Gonzo, but she was shocked by her writing.

Instead of adding to her current nonfiction piece, she had started a romance novel. The first three chapters were only a rough draft, but the story had a decent plot and memorable characters. Notably, the main character had a friend with sassy witticisms who reminded Ren of Gonzo.

"I must really miss him," she said aloud.

She typed a new message to her friend, apologizing. She asked him to call her, but she doubted he would do it. Gonzo was upset with her, so she'd have to track him down and apologize in person.

"Did you have a good night?"

Ren almost jumped out of her seat. She thought she was used to the way Jonas let himself in and out of the house, but she was so lost in her thoughts that she hadn't heard him come in. Since Gonzo had left, Jonas came in with his caretaker key. She didn't like it, but she avoided confrontation. When she left the lake house, she could avoid Jonas's calls and texts, but it would be uncomfortable to end things while she was staying next door.

"It was fine," she told him.

He rubbed a finger over her flushed face. "Who were you messaging?"

She looked down at the phone and showed him Gonzo's name. "I haven't heard from Gonzo since he left."

Jonas laughed dryly. "He realizes he was bested, so he hit the high road."

Ren popped out of her seat. "What?"

Jonas realized his mistake and attempted to backpedal. "I just meant that he must have liked you as more than friends, but when he saw us together—"

Ren's hand went to her hip. "He's gay, so I doubt he wants anything to do with me sexually."

Trying to maintain some peace, Jonas held his hands up. "There are some people who like both—"

"Not Gonzo," she returned. "He only likes men, and he'll be getting married soon."

She'd let the last part slip, and she regretted it. Jonas wasn't going to alert Blane to Gonzo's plan, but it was a secret Jonas didn't deserve to hear.

Jonas's eyebrows lifted. "I doubt it."

"What's that supposed to mean?"

Jonas ran a hand through his hair. "It's nothing." When he looked at her, his eyes were glassy. "I don't want to fight."

Ren dropped her gaze. "Me either."

He approached her cautiously, but when she allowed his touch, he brought her into his arms. His tongue explored her mouth, and he led her to the bed.

He reached for the drawer to pull out protection, but she grabbed his arm. "Remember? The last one had a hole in it. Do you have another one in your wallet?"

A strange look passed over his features, but he reached into his jeans and pulled out a condom. "We don't have to use one," he whispered, putting the package on the nightstand.

Ren reached for it, but he grabbed it before her, giving her an unsure smile. "I'm only kidding."

She settled onto the bed, letting his gentle caresses relax her. As he undressed her, watching her reaction to his movements, Ren reminded him she might still be sore from their last experience.

"Last night?" Jonas asked, pulling away from her.

Ren sat up in bed, instinctively grabbing the sheet to cover her nakedness. "Yeah. You were too rough with me last night, so just be a little more careful today."

He shot out of the bed, running a hand through his hair. He paced a few steps before he grabbed his jeans and shot his legs through them.

Surprised by her lover's abruptness, Ren jumped on the offensive. "It's okay. I liked it at the time, but—"

His icy glare cut her to her core. She sat on her knees, holding the sheet more tightly around her.

He stepped into his boots without speaking to her. Ren was shocked. *How could they go from a lovers' embrace to Jonas leaving in a frustrated frenzy?*

"What is it?" she demanded. "What did I do?"

He stopped at the bedroom door, his profile darkened by the shadows in the hall. "I wasn't here last night."

Ren called after him, but Jonas left quickly and resolutely. After the front door slammed, Ren laid back on her pillow, stunned.

If Jonas hadn't been with her last night, who had crawled into her bed?

She had been drunk, but she thought she knew enough about her lover to recognize his form and smell. Nothing had seemed off except for the way he had taken her, forcing her hands down when he flipped her onto her stomach.

Looking back, she never remembered Jonas treating her body with anything but tenderness. She had thought he was trying to spice things up, though. After all, creeping into her bed in the middle of the night was part of a fantasy she'd never known she'd had.

She'd had a passing thought that she had dreamed up the experience, but her soreness and the unused, leaky condom on her nightstand had proved that she'd been with someone. She had thought it was Jonas.

She shivered with the thought that someone else had taken advantage of her. *But who would have done it?*

The realization crashed into her so hard that she lost her breath. Part of her knew the truth, while the other part denied it.

Bile crept into her throat, and she coughed from the burn. She wrapped the sheet around her and ran to the bathroom, dropping it in the hall as she processed the deed had been done over the same sheet.

She made it to the shower before she threw up. Everything was bright red from the wine she'd drunk the previous night. Three glasses of wine shouldn't have made her so intoxicated that she didn't recognize Jonas.

But the other person had been a close match. He hadn't spoken, and he was gone as soon as she had fallen asleep.

Ren let the water run over her before she scrubbed her body. The heat of the water and the excess soap did nothing to make her feel clean. She finally bent down and held her knees, crying harder than the water that ran over her.

Riley. How could she not have known it was Riley?

CHAPTER 31

R en didn't believe in abortion. She'd had a friend in high school whose parents had made her terminate her untimely pregnancy, and she'd seen the result. Her friend had been an emotional wreck and had tried to commit suicide twice before she'd succeeded.

Ren looked into adoption agencies online. She couldn't imagine having a child in the world who didn't know she existed, so she searched for open adoptions. She only found one agency she liked, and she couldn't explain the reason she thought it was best. She just had a good feeling about it as soon as she read the wording on their home page. *Your child will be loved,* their motto promised.

That was important to Ren. Her child should be loved. The baby wasn't responsible for her bad decision and Kai's impulses, so he'd be able to enjoy all the love and support he deserved.

Ren had felt the baby was a boy since she found out she was pregnant. She refused to hear the sex, though, even though a nurse had cautioned her to find out the gender so she could prepare for the baby's arrival. She'd wanted to be surprised, and even though she was seriously considering giving her baby to a loving family, Ren still wanted to experience every part of her pregnancy.

Kai was excited about the pregnancy, but they only talked about it when she brought it up. The exception was on Sunday nights.

Ren's due date was on a Sunday, so she turned another week pregnant on that day. On Sundays, Kai would put her feet into his lap and massage them as he read about the development of their baby for that week. He had downloaded an app that told him about the focus on particular organs and systems. He encouraged her to put the same app on her phone, but Ren preferred her paperback pregnancy book.

Kai was happy on Sunday nights, as he rubbed circles around her arches and grew surprised over the speed of the heartbeat or the development of little fingers and toes. He still shouted at Ren and complained about the neglected housework, but he was having more good days than bad days. At night, he held his hand over her belly as if he were protecting the baby from harm.

He told her the names he had considered, Josh for a boy and Della for a girl, but Ren didn't want to name the baby after either of Kai's parents. She maintained the peace, though, and smiled, making no commitment.

He glanced at the gender-neutral clothes she picked up at the stores, but he mumbled about their expense as she walked away. Ren wondered if her husband had truly been ready for the emotional and financial support a child needed, and she decided he hadn't thought it through at all. Since she had been caught up in their Christmas moment, too, she tried not to hold him accountable for some of his anxiousness.

Ren's reprieves came every weekend. Kai would pack up his clothes and diving suit on Friday mornings, and he'd leave for the lake immediately after work. Whether it was sunny or raining, Kai never altered his plans.

When he left on Friday mornings, kissing the top of her head before he hurried out the door, Ren's anxieties left with him. She felt free to move around the house, and she wrote pages of her manuscript without the fear of performing for him.

When Kai was home, Ren was on edge. Even when he strutted into the house on Sunday evenings, she was aware the slightest misstep could cause him to erupt.

It was confusing, as before the accident, Kai had been kind to her, always thinking of ways to make her happy. Now, she rushed to be certain everything was clean and in its place.

Kai had a routine that helped him remember things. He put his keys and workbag in the same place every afternoon, and his bathroom was arranged methodically.

Her husband still prepared their meals, but he couldn't always remember the dishes that went best together. He once served her beets and peanut butter, and another time, he forgot what accompanied dressing, so a rainbow of condiments decorated the table.

Kai reported good progress from his therapist, but given the circumstances at home, she was unconvinced. She called the therapist's office, and because of Kia's HIPPA documents that released information to her, Ren found out Kai had stopped all therapy after only five months.

Ren questioned the receptionist, but the lady could only read the notes on her husband's file. She left a message for the doctor, and after a week, Ren received a phone call from the therapist.

Kai was at work, but he was due home in an hour. Ren found out more about her husband in her fifteen-minute conversation with the therapist than she had since he came home from the hospital.

Kai was doing well until he hit a roadblock. During an exercise, Kai had forgotten the names of several common objects. He could laugh it off, but he forgot them again when he returned the following week. The next week, he was unable to recall another set of objects that were commonplace.

The therapist had witnessed his frustration during the exercises, and when she mentioned the first signs of aphasia, Kia had flown into a rage. He'd debased her degree and refused to consider further treatment.

The therapist encouraged Ren to help Kia find a professional who was equipped to handle his worsening condition. Ren knew her efforts would not be appreciated, though. She needed help.

Kai's parents were dead, so she had to find people he liked and trusted for an intervention. She called his roommate from college and his work partner, but she wondered if it would be enough to help him see he needed help. Kai was a social man, and he knew many people, but he didn't have many deep friendships.

Kai's past roommate responded immediately. He hadn't heard from Kai since the accident, but he was eager to help.

Kai's partner, Bentley, was a little less enthusiastic. He cited conflicting schedules and family obligations until Ren reminded him that Kai's mental state could impact their firm. He was more available after he thought about his future profits.

Three weeks after speaking to the therapist, Ren prepared for Kai's intervention. She called the neurologist, but she wasn't on the HIPPA form at the office, so the doctor couldn't speak to her.

She asked some general questions, and she provided Ren with information about the possible effects of Kai's injury.

Ren shopped for snacks and wine and picked up crackers and ginger ale for herself. When she pulled into the driveway, she carried the snacks to the front room through the front door. It was a more direct route than the garage.

A car stopped behind her, and a man got out. Ren tried not to notice him yelling at the driver or kicking the car, but it was quite a scene. The car sped off, leaving the man in the middle of the road, screaming a string of obscenities. Ren was almost at the door when the man called to her.

"That was some show, huh?"

Ren turned to him and smiled, not wishing to upset him more from a nonresponse. She regretted her decision when he jogged up to her. He ran through the yard, oblivious to the sidewalks on either side of him.

"You're Lauren, right?" he said.

She nodded, and a vague memory of his face at one of Kai's barbeques came to mind. "My name is Ren." She searched for something pleasant to add. "I met you last summer, didn't I?"

"Gonzo," he reminded her.

He shoved his hands in his pockets and looked at her bag. "Are you pregnant?"

The answer to his question was clear as she colored and moved her mouth. After nothing followed, Gonzo smiled and lifted her burden from her arms.

He pointed to the crackers and ginger ale on top. "My mom swore by that combination. She had a severe case of morning sickness when she was pregnant with me. Something like—" He searched for the term and shook his head when it wasn't forthcoming.

"I've heard of it," Ren offered. "I don't remember what it's called either."

"How far along are you?"

Ren's hands shook as she searched for the right key. Even though she'd just witnessed Gonzo's hostile display, she felt like he was a good person, but she was concerned about letting him into her home.

She found the key and opened the door. "I'm almost five months."

He looked at her belly and let out a low whistle. "Girl, you're hidin' it well. There are a lot of women who blow up as soon as they find out."

Ren directed Gonzo to a table by the door, and she unloaded the bag. "I'm keeping it a secret until I'm ready."

Gonzo's skin formed a crease above his nose. "Why? You're past twelve weeks, and that's usually when—"

She cleared her throat, interrupting him. "I have my reasons."

He nodded. "You sound like my ex. He always *had his reasons*." He put air quotes around the last three words.

Ren motioned out the window. "Was that him?"

Gonzo chuckled. "No, my dear, innocent child. That was my beaux for the evening. He wasn't happy with a one-and-done."

"It looked like you were the one who wasn't happy," Ren commented. She closed her eyes, realizing she had crossed a line.

Gonzo laughed and nudged her arm. "You're a sassy little thing, aren't you?" He pointed to the picture of Ren and Kai on their wedding day. "It's nice to see that Mr. Wonderful hasn't broken you yet."

"I thought you liked Kai."

He took the wine out of the box and surveyed it. "I don't have to like a man to go to his house and drink his alcohol. Speaking of which, this is garbage. You should give it to me and spare your guests the sour experience."

Ren was confident in her choice of wine, but she consented to Gonzo taking it. There was another bottle in the refrigerator.

"They should be here any minute," she told Gonzo, hoping he'd take the hint.

Gonzo kissed both her cheeks. "Well, unless it's an orgy, and you plan on leaving me with hunky men, I'll be on my way."

Before she could respond, he walked to the door. "My mom used to make ginger soup for me when I was sick. She said she used it when she was pregnant. I'll try to find the recipe."

Then he was gone. When she looked out the window, he was strutting down the sidewalk, putting the bottle to his mouth. She thought it might have been for show, as he hadn't opened the bottle before he'd left.

Ren flew into action, fluffing pillows and making sure her appearance was acceptable. Within five minutes, Bentley pulled into the driveway, and before he got out of his car, Kai's roommate glided up to the curb.

Bentley and Dylan walked up the sidewalk together. Ren was glad she didn't have to introduce them, as they had met in college and often spoke to each other during Kai's parties.

Ren greeted them soberly, and they hugged her. It crossed her mind that the men would treat her with more kindness if she told them she was pregnant, but it went against her ideals. They should see her as a strong woman who wanted the best for her husband, not a female who needed their protection.

Dylan's open smile lit up the room, and he walked around the room, looking at photographs and striking up polite conversation. Bentley sat in an oversized chair. Other than responding to Dylan's questions, he hardly looked up from his phone.

"What exactly are we supposed to do?" he said.

Ren glanced at Dylan and noticed he was waiting for her response. "I hope we can talk Kai into accepting his condition and going back into a treatment program."

Bentley glanced up from his screen. "You know him, right? Have you been living with the same man I work with every day?"

"I know he has some pride—"

Bentley scoffed.

"Now we can't go jumpin' the gun," Dylan piped up. "Lauren was right to call us here. If there's a chance we can help Kai, then I'm all in."

Ren cringed when he said the name Kai called her. She opened her mouth to correct the misconception when she saw a car in the window. Recognizing her husband's vehicle, she broke into a cold sweat.

Dylan put his hand on her back. "It's okay. We're here to help."

Ren thought she saw Bentley roll his eyes. Whatever his feelings were, he put up his cell phone and leaned back into the chair.

Ren opened the door for Kai and led him to the front room. He must have thought she was trying to seduce him, for he came with her easily enough, but when he saw his two friends, his face reshuffled.

"Hey, guys. Did my wife plan a party?"

Ren's heart went out to him, but she had to get through the intervention. She owed it to Dylan and Bentley to keep the meeting as short as possible, so she got to the point.

"We're worried about you, sweetheart."

His eyebrows went up. "Why?"

Ren gathered her courage and kept talking. "You're forgetting things more often, from case dates to where we keep the spices, and I called your therapist—"

He laughed, dropping his bag and sitting in a chair across from Bentley. "She was a therapist assigned by the hospital. She was just trying to create more problems to keep me in therapy."

"I've heard about that," Bentley acknowledged.

The two men exchanged a glance, and it irritated Ren. "How about the Gouge case? Did Kai remember everything he needed for it?"

The Gouge case was the one that had caused Bentley to ask Kai to take a break. Ren had expected him to back her up, but Bentley adopted another approach.

"It's all water under the bridge."

Ren regretted asking Bentley to come to the intervention. She was even more upset when the two men fist-bumped.

Dylan noticed her distress and jumped in. "Ren has some concerns, and I've been wonderin' why you haven't called me."

"I've been busy," he said, chuckling with Bentley. "You may have chosen the calm life of an accountant, but Bentley and I stay covered up with work all week."

Dylan was undeterred by the jab at his profession. "That never stopped you before. You used to call me on a lunch break every other week, and we'd hang out once a month."

"He's been going to the lake," Ren cut in. "He's not had time for anyone."

It was a low blow, but she was angry with her husband for alienating her concerns. He called her out on it immediately.

"That's not fair, Lauren. You told me I could go every weekend."

"Maybe I thought it wouldn't last so long." She hated the tears that glazed her vision.

Kai stood up and shook his head. "I'm sorry you guys had to be here for something that seems to be a bored housewife's plea for attention." He addressed Dylan. "I didn't realize we hadn't spoken in a while, but I'll be sure to catch up with you more often."

He crossed the distance between them and hugged Dylan. "Say 'hello' to Marty for me."

Bentley took it as his cue to make a speedy getaway, and he threw out waves as he went out the front door. Kai gently led Dylan in the same direction, making promises to see him in the coming weeks.

Once the men were gone, Ren felt her knees buckle. She made it to a chair and sat.

Kai's back was to her as he spoke. "If you only knew."

His words were a little muffled, and Ren asked him to repeat them. He turned around and glared at her.

"You need to think about where you want to live," he told her.

Ren had expected his anger, but she hadn't believed he would send her away for trying to help him. She could only sit on the chair with wide eyes as her husband took deliberate steps toward her.

"Do you want to live in a nice house with a baby and a husband?" He paused, hoping to draw out an effect. "Or do you want to go back to your parent's house alone?"

Ren didn't even twitch. Kai's voice was venomous, and she knew there was more.

"I specialize in family law," he went on, "and if you think you'll ever see that baby again after I divorce you, you're wrong."

He stormed out of the room, and she heard the shower running. After a few moments, she felt steady enough to walk to the kitchen on shaky legs.

Ren poured a glass of water and settled in front of the television. She stared at the blank screen, and she hardly registered it when Kai turned it on. He didn't prepare dinner, and he didn't offer to read the baby's progress to her or rub her feet.

He sat with her but on a different couch, and sometimes she thought she saw menacing stares in her peripheral vision. It was almost like she was sitting in the same room as a murderer who was sharpening his knife.

It was then that Ren decided Kai would not have the chance to father the baby. Even if it meant giving up all her rights and the possibility of knowing the child, her baby would never know the man his father had become.

CHAPTER 32

"I 've not seen him," Blane said. "I thought he was still with you."

After not receiving a response from Gonzo for another week, Ren reached out to Blane. Conveniently, his number was listed on his social media account.

"Where is he then?"

"He may have taken a trip somewhere," Blane said, clearly not as affected by Gonzo's abrupt absence as Ren. "He's always talking about getting away."

"But he's never done it."

There was a pause before he said, "It'll be good for him. I'll call you if I hear from him."

They hung up, and Ren was presented with a new problem. *Had her friend finally taken the vacation he'd hinted at for years, or was he missing?*

Jonas couldn't take her mind off Gonzo. He tried to soothe her worries, but he had little experience with driving away her anxieties.

Ren wished he'd go home. She was tired of his forced companionship, but she didn't have the nerve to tell him. It seemed Kai's death had changed her in that way, too.

Ren hadn't been with many people, but the men she had dated never broke up with her. She could sense the decline in the relationship, and she would write a sorrowful note to them, explaining that their differences were too numerous to continue.

Her writing had been eloquent and her desire for their happiness was clear, so she had remained friends with all her past lovers. There were never ill feelings, and most of them would have eagerly returned to a more intimate relationship with her.

There was something about Jonas that led her to believe he wouldn't be as kind about a breakup. Even though he'd said he wanted to take it slow, he'd practically moved in with her.

Jonas had taken one of the bottom drawers in the dresser and put in some of his clothes. She was genuinely irritated when she'd noted the addition of a couple of pairs of jeans and a few shirts, but she was even more upset when his body wash and loofa made an appearance in her shower. She would have been okay if he had brought over a toothbrush or a shaving kit, but making his own drawer without consulting her was a bit much.

"I have to stay at my house tonight," he announced.

His news softened her spirits, and she put aside the laptop she'd been holding. She had only typed a few paragraphs, but it was for the continuation of her romance, not the project that was due in less than three months.

He moved next to her, putting an arm around her shoulders. "I'll be back tomorrow morning."

Ren stared up at him benignly. He placed a kiss on her nose, but when she didn't turn away, he pulled her on top of him and kissed her deeply.

Jonas picked her up and carried her to the bedroom, laying her gently on the bed. His hands moved down her body, exploring her in the ways he learned she enjoyed.

Ren broke their contact to grab protection from the drawer. She'd ordered another box, and they'd arrived just in time.

When she handed it to Jonas, liquid seeped into her palm. She sat up in bed, examining the package.

She studied the foil and found a small, round hole in the center. It seemed too perfect to have been an error by the company. She grabbed another one, and it confirmed her suspicions.

Ren looked at Jonas. "Did you poke a hole in the condoms?"

He didn't answer her, and his face went white, confirming her suspicions. She threw the condom at him, and it bounced off his shoulder.

"How dare you!"

Ren catapulted off the bed and went straight to the bottom drawer of her dresser. She slung his clothes onto the bed, narrowly missing him with each article she threw.

"Get out!"

Jonas didn't move. He remained on the bed with tears in his eyes. "Ren, please."

"Please what?" she yelled. Her voice bordered on hysterical, but she felt she had every reason to feel the way she did. "You poked holes in the condoms! What kind of crazy man does that?"

His eyes darkened. "Don't call me crazy."

Ren had to hold herself back. She wanted desperately to repeat the word in a chant until he left, but she took a deep breath.

The reason for his deception was obvious, and she chose to address it. "Why do you want to get me pregnant?"

"Because I love you." His response was automatic.

Ren threw up her hands. "You don't love me! Aside from reading my books and spending the past month with me, what do you really know about me?"

Jonas got up off the bed. "I know you like to be alone, but you get lonely. I know you twist your tongue and chew on it while you work, and I know you deserve to be loved."

Jonas was sincere, and it took the edge off her temper. She was still angry, but his arms felt good around her.

"I'm sorry," he went on. "I never should have tried to get you pregnant without your consent. It was wrong."

She wanted to cite other reasons his deception bothered her, but the tears on her shoulders stopped her. He wouldn't let her look at him as he cried. He shielded his eyes with his hand.

"I'm so sorry," he said again. "I was just afraid you'd leave, and I'd never see you again."

"I think we need some time apart." Ren pulled herself away.

This time, Jonas wasn't afraid to show his emotions. "No. I know what that means." He motioned to the bed where the sheets still held ripples from the motion of their bodies. "We were just—" He dropped his hand and head. "I ruined it. I ruined everything."

Ren couldn't stand to hurt another person. She'd felt that pain once, and it was so terrible that she never wanted to be the reason another person felt pain.

She drew him into her arms. She held him as he cried, not knowing the right thing to say.

After minutes that seemed like an hour, Jonas wiped his face and went to the bathroom. When he returned with a blotchy face and bright green, red-rimmed eyes, their conversation seemed to be forgotten, conveniently swept under the rug where he kept the rest of the issues that bothered him.

"I'm going to go," he announced, moving into the doorway. "I'll be back tomorrow morning."

He turned around, but before he was out of her sight, he stopped. "I love you."

He waited for her to return the sentiment, but when he heard nothing, he left, shutting the door softly behind him.

CHAPTER 33

"**D**on't get me wrong," Becky said, "those boys are beautiful, but they're bat-crap crazy."

"I don't use that term," Ren told her politely. "There's such a stigma around mental health—"

"And that's another thing," Becky went on, undeterred. "Both of them have some sort of" —she held her fingers up in air quotes— "*thing* they inherited from their mother. She was bipolar or had a split personality." She took a drink of her wine as she tried to recall. "I can't remember."

After the story she'd heard from Jonas about his childhood, Ren wasn't surprised by Becky's gossip. No mother should ever have done to her children what that woman did to her sons.

"Multiple personalities!" Becky shouted suddenly, startling Ren. She nodded and relaxed in her chair, congratulating herself with another sip of wine.

"That doesn't mean they inherited her condition," Ren spoke carefully.

Becky rolled her eyes. "Look at the signs." She held up a finger. "They isolate themselves. I mean, no one has actually seen Riley for years."

"I thought you said he tried to run your husband over with a boat?"

Becky put her empty wine glass on the table. "That was ages ago. I haven't seen that boy since—" She looked off and smiled.

"Since you slept with him?" Ren guessed.

Becky's grin widened. "I guess he has a reason for avoiding me," she admitted.

The woman leaned forward in her chair, a faraway look in her eyes. "I was going to leave my husband for that boy, but then Jonas's girlfriend disappeared, and—"

"Wait!" Ren threw up her hand. "I thought she left him."

Becky nodded, accepting the wine Ren poured into her glass. "Yeah. But no one has heard from her since."

"Isn't she on social media?"

Becky patted her hand. "Not everybody is a fan of that stuff. She was young, but I think she didn't want her parents to know what she was doing all the time."

"She was an adult. Why does it matter what her parents thought?"

Becky snorted and held her wine out so she wouldn't spill it on herself. Of course, she had no concern for the light-colored flooring.

"He didn't tell you, did he?" She waited for effect before she continued. "Jonas loves the young ones. I think you're the oldest person he's ever been with."

Ren reached for the question that bothered her the most. "How old was Colette?"

Becky drew out her next drink, prolonging the suspense. Ren wanted to shake the woman, but she waited.

"She was seventeen."

Ren decided not to answer the door. She locked the deadbolt, as Jonas's key only worked for the lock on the knob.

She stared at it for a long time, as if her action would alert him and bring him running to the door.

She couldn't leave yet. There was one thing she still had to do, and she would not leave without doing it.

She moved from one room to another, throwing items into boxes. The wine she'd shared with Becky made her dizzy, so she napped into the early evening.

She woke when a boat sped too close to her dock. The speed limit was strict in the residential area, and she cursed the driver. She assumed teenagers were out on the water.

As the sun dimmed, blue lights flashed across the living room walls. She stood up and peered across the lake.

Just on the other side, boats and people were gathered on a neighbor's dock. A police officer and a man dressed in plain clothes shouted to a crowd of twenty people.

"That's Becky's house," she said out loud. "I hope nothing has happened to her."

Her neighbor was annoying, but she was likable. She gossiped, but she didn't cause harm to anyone.

Ren racked her brain for anything Becky may have mentioned about her day. The wine had made their conversation fuzzy, but she thought she remembered Becky saying that she was going to try swimming in the water. Ren hadn't believed it was warm enough, but a rash of eighty-degree days around Easter caused Becky to believe the temperature was just right for her.

Ren watched the dock, wondering if she should join the people on the other side. It would be a relief to see Becky among the crowd, but it would mean something had happened to another poor soul. After all, the crowd was gathered for a reason.

She'd just decided to walk over when she spotted Jonas. His bright white button-up and cowboy boots were unmistakable. She wondered if Riley was in the mix of people on the dock.

Ren made a sandwich, even though she could hardly eat it, and packed boxes into the car. She felt comfortable going back and forth between her house and vehicle, as she knew Jonas had joined the efforts of whatever alarm had been raised on the other side of the lake.

There was room in her car for two or three more boxes, but she was so tired she could barely hold up her head. She had never gone to sleep so early after a nap, but even though it wasn't midnight, she had worked hard all evening. She dragged the rest of the bottle of wine up the stairs with her, but it remained on the dresser, untouched.

As she brushed her teeth, she tried to recall if she'd bolted the door. She crept down the stairs slowly, as her dizziness only allowed small steps.

"I'm going to slow down," she promised herself, her voice cutting through the night. "My drinking is getting out of hand."

The door wasn't bolted, but she pushed the lock in place. Satisfied that her boyfriend wouldn't be able to surprise her with a sexual experience he would deny later, Ren climbed the stairs. It seemed it took her forever to reach her room, and when she did, she flicked the light and fell onto the bed.

Deep in the night, Ren thought she heard a woman screaming. She rolled over and looked around the room. Nothing seemed out of place, but her brain nagged her to look more closely. Her vision blurred, and Ren's head fell back onto her pillow.

Once she was asleep, he moved out of the shadows and stared at her. Her dark hair made a curtain over her face. She was pale and frail, just like the others. Just like his mother.

He pulled the blanket up to her shoulder. She wouldn't feel it or know he'd been there.

Drugging her wine had been a brilliant idea, but he always had the best ideas. He paved the way for Jonas to take her the way he liked, but he treated her like he was going to marry her one day. The wine kept her too disoriented to concentrate on the noises in the basement, though, and that was enough for him.

He wasn't going to let some sniveling woman ruin his game. He'd been playing it for years, sometimes by himself and sometimes with others, but it wasn't going to stop just because she wanted to sell the house.

No.

She could disappear. And when everyone thought she was just another casualty of the lake, he could admire her in his collection.

CHAPTER 34

It was already past noon when Ren woke. She sat up and rubbed her eyes, throwing off the blanket she must have pulled over herself in the night.

She wondered if Jonas had already tried the door and found it bolted. It was a good possibility, but she didn't care. She had the perfect excuse to leave him, and she doubted she'd ever see him again after she left the lake.

Ren didn't want to be in a romantic relationship again anytime soon. She'd leave Jonas behind and wait a couple of years before she dived back into the dating pool. She'd let her desires and emotions get the best of her, but she was ready to break free.

Ren took a shower and put on a pot of coffee. As she drank her first cup, she stared out at Becky's dock. No one was there, and the lake was quiet.

She wondered if she had witnessed a search team and if Becky was okay. She wanted to call her, but she didn't have her phone number.

She looked up the names and addresses of families around the lake, but she only found one she knew. Mathes.

Ren sighed deeply, remembering her last conversation with them. It could be embarrassing, but they didn't know her phone number, so she could pretend to be someone else. She dialed the number, and when it rang, she hoped for the best.

Augusta's mother answered, and Ren launched into her story.

"Hello, Mrs. Mathes. I got your number online. I ordered some products from Becky, but I can't find her number. Do you have it?"

There was a strained silence on the other end of the line. "How did you say you got my number?"

Ren almost hung up the phone, but she reminded herself that the woman didn't know her identity.

"I searched for people who lived close to Becky, and I found your number."

She scoffed. "No doubt it was attached to a missing person article."

"Maybe," Ren hedged. "But that's not why I'm calling—"

"I think that's exactly why you're callin'!" the woman yelled. "You and your reporter friends can back off. We have nothing to say about the similarities between the cases."

The call ended, and Ren put her phone on the counter. She'd thought her cover story was good, but she wasn't a convincing liar.

The tapping brought her back to reality. At first, it was only a slight noise, but after a heartbeat, it grew to a knocking that almost rattled the pipes in her kitchen sink.

Tired of cowering, Ren stormed to the basement door and slung it open. It gave easily in her grasp.

As she took the first step into the basement, keys rattled in the front door. In one swift movement, she backed up and closed the door gently.

Creeping to the front window, she peered out onto the porch. Jonas stood at her door, running a hand through his hair and holding a bottle of wine. It was too early to drink, so she assumed he had anticipated resuming their arrangement.

She stepped away from the window, watching for his shadow to move. He stood there for a while, trying his key twice more and knocking loudly.

She could imagine his dismay and the distress he felt. *Could she really leave him outside without an explanation?*

She went to the door with every intention of opening it, but she heard his footsteps echoing off the porch steps. It seemed she'd avoided an uncomfortable conversation. She doubted she'd be as lucky next time. She could almost imagine him camping on her porch until she answered the door.

"This is ridiculous!" she said, throwing up her hands. "Why can't he just take a hint!"

Frustration took hold of her and she grabbed her car keys. She could throw a few things into a bag and leave quickly.

By the time she had packed her clothes, her temper had cooled. She walked her bag out to the car, but she wasn't as fiercely determined to leave. She still had something to do.

"Going somewhere?"

Ren almost jumped out of her skin at the sound of his voice. It seemed she hadn't been too far from the truth when she'd imagined him camped out on her porch.

Jonas ran a hand through his hair and shifted the flowers he was holding from one hand to the other. "I was afraid you'd leave. It's the same thing Colette did when I found out about her and my brother."

"I didn't sleep with your brother."

He raised his eyebrows. "Really? Because it wasn't me who pinned your arms to the bed."

It occurred to Ren that she hadn't discussed the details with him. She relayed that fact, and Jonas grew flustered.

"H-He told me," he stuttered. "He said you liked it, and I was too afraid to—"

"Cut the crap! I know your brother didn't come back from his trip. You just use him to live out your fantasies."

"I wasn't there that night," he said coldly.

A realization hit Ren like she had been shot in the back. "Why do you have to leave on certain days?" She waited for the surprise to register across his features. "Do you go to therapy?"

Ren advanced a step, confident that she was on the right track. "Is that why your brother left? Did he see the signs of your mother's illness in you?"

"Shut up!"

It was the first time he'd ever yelled at her, and it scared her. She was acutely aware she was in a secluded section of the woods with an unstable man.

He threw the flowers on the ground. "Sometimes you make me so mad I could—"

Ren took a step back and tripped on a tree root. She scrambled to get up, and Jonas's expression changed as he watched her struggle.

He approached her with his palms up. "Can I help you up?"

"No," Ren answered, finally finding her footing.

They stared at each other. Ren had nothing more to say to him.

Jonas picked up the flowers and dusted them off. He tried to hand them to her, but she wouldn't take them.

"Riley left," he said, "but it wasn't because of me. He had his own stuff to sift through, and he came back five years ago."

Ren didn't believe anything he said. She listened and hoped he would provide her with an opportunity to get away from him.

"Kai saw him," he added. "They used to go out on the boat together all the time."

She spoke with a knee-jerk response. "My husband never mentioned your brother. He only talked about you."

Jonas ran a hand through his hair and laughed dryly. "Riley's secretive. He's at the house now. I can take you to him." He looked up hopefully.

Ren shook her head. "I don't think so."

The flowers fell from his hand again. "Yeah. It might be a little awkward after what happened."

He stared down at her and sighed. "If you want to see me, you know where to find me." He shrugged. "If not, I guess I have to understand."

Ren felt much better about his reaction, and it emboldened her. Before he left, she chanced a question.

"What were you doing on Becky's dock yesterday?"

"She's missing," he yelled back, without stopping his feet. "They found her boat and a float, but they can't find her. She's probably dead."

The tone of his voice chilled her to her marrow. He spoke with such a finality that Ren thought he knew exactly where to find Becky. And, most likely, she was dead.

CHAPTER 35

Ren talked herself out of the thoughts that led her to believe her lover was a murderer. The bright sunshine and the thought that she'd be sleeping in her own bed that night helped her dismiss the creepy edge to his voice as he had relayed the news about their neighbor.

Ren sat in front of a blank sheet of paper. When she was in college, her marketing professor told her that the best way to write a letter was to start with something nice, tell the bad news, and wrap it up with something positive. She had written the letters to her adult lovers using that format, but as she sat in the afternoon sun on the back deck, she couldn't think of anything positive to say.

I like having sex with you, wasn't quite what she wanted to express, but it was the only thing that came to mind. He was pretty handy, and most of the time, he was nice to her, but Jonas didn't have the same qualities as her other lovers. He didn't make her laugh or feel loved, and his interests were different from hers. In a way, he made her feel protected, but that was the best she could do.

Finally, she penned the note.

```
Dear Jonas,

Our time together has been a whirlwind of
fantastic physical experiences. I'm glad we met.

I have to go back to my house. I know you
don't want me to leave, but the trust in our
relationship has been broken, and I can't move
forward with you in my life.

I hope you understand and won't take it too
hard. I appreciate your loyalty and kindness,
and I know you'll make someone happy one day.


Your friend,
Ren
```

Satisfied with her work, she sighed deeply. She walked inside and placed the notebook on the kitchen table.

She spent the next hour throwing memories into boxes. She didn't plan to come back after she left, so she took everything she thought Kia's extended family would want.

She traveled into the spare room for extra boxes and went through the closet. She found Kia's parents' wedding clothes and a wet suit.

After examining it, she realized it was hers. Kia had brought it to the lake house in hopes she would dive with him one day. She had come up to the lake house for it, but now that the suit was in her hands, she felt shaky and cold.

"You don't have to put it on," she said aloud.

Ren ran her hand over the suit. She had an air tank in the car, as she'd anticipated the possibility of diving.

"You don't have to do it," she told herself. "You can put it away and never look at it again."

But she knew she wouldn't.

Ren stood at the hole. She wasn't in her dive suit yet, as it had taken some stealth to sneak past Jonas's house.

The house had been silent, and Jonas's truck had been gone, but that didn't mean that Riley was gone —if he'd ever been there— or that Jonas's truck would stay gone. She went from tree to tree, hoping the long afternoon shadows would keep her hidden as she went to the private swimming hole at the edge of their property.

Once the house had disappeared from her sight, she breathed a sigh of relief. She'd think about the best way to get back to the lake house later. For now, she had to face her fear.

Ren could easily have gone to her dock and taken a boat to the middle of the lake, diving back into the water. Something about it didn't seem right, though. Perhaps it was all the people who could watch her as she tried to master her fear. She couldn't imagine being on display as she tried to overcome her debilitating anxiety about going into the water.

She put on the suit, secured her equipment, and stared at the water. She had picked up a flashlight for dives in murky water, but she doubted she'd need it. It was a comfort, though. *What made her think she could dive more easily than she could swim?*

Maybe she felt the wet suit protected her, or perhaps the oxygen strapped to her back provided a lifeline. She put all her thoughts away, compartmentalizing them into little boxes that she banged shut. The only information she allowed herself to register was what she had to do in order to dip herself into the water.

She hardly looked at its glassy surface, opting to go in feet first, as she didn't want to fall backward and hit her head on a rock. When she plunged into the water, silence engulfed her.

For a few heartbeats, she was a frightened mess, but once she regulated her breathing, she felt the same feeling wash over her she had when she'd drifted away from her ocean exploration group years ago.

Silence.

It wasn't soundproof, as she could still hear herself breathe, but she was in stillness. The dark water engulfed her, hiding her existence from the world. No one could find her here, as they wouldn't know where to look. She didn't have to deal with her husband's death, Jonas's insecure attachment to her, or...

She stopped, willing her mind away from the incident that kept her in fear of the water. Many people thought it was the accident, but Ren could have jumped back into her pool the next month. What happened to her was deeper, and it almost killed her.

CHAPTER 36

Kai didn't talk about the failed intervention. In many ways it should have been a warning to her, but she chose to believe he wasn't fighting with her because she was pregnant.

She was still nervous, as he hadn't spoken to her since his friends left. When he fixed spaghetti and poured a bottle of wine, she couldn't eat.

"Drink your wine then," he said, motioning to the full glass.

"I'm pregnant."

"You can drink one glass," he replied around a mouthful of food. "The doctor said."

Ren regretted telling him what her obstetrician had told her. She looked at her food sulkily.

"How would you know? You're never there."

There was a sharp intake of breath. The silence that followed was almost painful as she waited for his reaction.

"Someone has to work."

"I work," she shot back. "My last book paid off the car."

Kai hadn't used finances in an argument with her until that moment. It hurt her, but his insinuation that she didn't contribute to the household enraged her.

"We both know who makes the money around here," he said calmly, without looking up from his meal.

Ren didn't feel like cowering. She decided it was time to either have better communication with her husband or have the fight she'd been dreading since she'd organized an intervention.

"And how long will you be able to bring in money if your memory goes? The therapist said aphasia—"

She'd hardly gotten the word out of her mouth before Kai's hand shot out. He grabbed her by the neck, increasing the pressure as he saw the fear in her eyes.

"I could snap you like a twig, and no one would miss you," he said. "If they did, they wouldn't know where to find you."

Ren wished she could blame his temper on the wine, but he'd only drunk half a glass. She could still breathe, but it was getting harder.

"The baby," she squeaked out.

His head tilted as he considered her plea. "There is that."

His fingers released slowly. She coughed and gagged as Kai finished his meal, completely unaffected. As she sputtered, the few bites of food she'd taken came up and covered her lap.

Kai got up and took his plate to the sink. When he returned to the table, he surveyed her.

"You're a mess. You need to clean up."

Ren jumped at the excuse of getting away from him. She ran upstairs and grabbed some clothes. Normally, she would have pulled out a pair of silk pajamas or lingerie, but she grabbed maternity leggings and a large shirt.

She heard Kai rustling around the kitchen as she prepared for a bath. He washed dishes as she rinsed out her clothes, and a tune carried up the stairs. It was an old song about a train she'd heard played in a popular movie.

The bath was warm and inviting. It didn't relax her, but it gave Ren an excuse to stay away from her husband, as a shower would have only given her mere minutes of freedom. She closed her eyes and leaned back on the lip of the tub.

That was it, she thought. *I can't stay with him after he tried to choke me.*

She couldn't just think of herself anymore, but she doubted she would have stayed if she'd not been pregnant. No one had ever been so violent with her up to that point, and every fiber of her being screamed for her to leave, but she knew she had to be smart about it.

Sure, he was a big-time lawyer in the town, and he'd destroy her in a courtroom, but there were other lawyers who were just as good as him. She'd find one and have their case moved to another county. She was pretty certain it was possible. Unfortunately, even though he had turned into an abuser, he would receive visitation rights to the baby, but she thought she might be able to draw out the divorce long enough to use his memory against him. At best, she hoped that sighting aphasia and demanding a mental evaluation would force the court to grant him only supervised visitation.

She rubbed her hand over her stomach. She couldn't wait to feel the baby move. She'd thought she'd felt bubbles a couple of times, but she dismissed it as gas. She longed for the days when she could feel a tiny arm or leg and she'd know the baby was okay.

For now, there was nothing. She briefly wondered if Kai had killed their unborn child with the stress of the past weeks. She wanted to give the baby up for adoption, but she needed her child to live.

When she'd researched her idea more, she'd learned that Kai would have to sign the adoption papers. She concocted fantasies where he wouldn't know she'd given birth, and she'd give the baby to a loving couple before he could do anything about it. But Kai would have found out about her deception, and he would have known what to do to get the baby back and keep Ren from ever seeing him.

A sound at the door jolted her out of her thoughts. A card slid between the lock and the frame, and the door popped open.

Kai let himself in quickly with a tray balanced on his hand. He scooted a bath stool near the tub and sat on it, holding the tray near her. It held her full glass of wine, a plate of crackers, and a card.

Ren sat up in the tub and accepted the hand towel he offered her. She took a sip of the wine, as she didn't want to upset him, and her throat was parched from vomiting.

Kai remained silent as Ren chewed a cracker and took another sip of wine. The crackers were dry, and the wine did little to coat them when she swallowed.

Ren opened the card, knowing it was an attempt at an apology she wouldn't truly accept. She pulled a lovely card from a golden envelope. It was an anniversary card, even though their anniversary was a couple of days away.

She read the words he didn't mean and tried to smile at appropriate intervals. The only addition to the card was his signature.

Ren closed the card and placed it on the tray. "Thank you, but our anniversary isn't for—"

"I know that," he snapped at her. He rubbed his eyes with his fingers. "I just thought it'd be a nice gesture after what happened."

She looked at the water. It just covered her stomach, coming to rest at the bottom of her breasts.

"You aren't the same," she said.

"I know."

Ren waited for more. She wished Kai would admit he was experiencing memory loss and needed help. If he could get on the track for treatment, she'd be there for him.

When the silence had dragged on for several minutes, Ren spoke. "I love you, Kai, and I only want you to get better."

He shot up, the tray and its contents spilling on the rug. "Better than what?" His eyes were wild with fury. "I'm the best I've ever been!"

As he stared at her, Ren calculated her next move. Naked in a tub of lukewarm water, she felt more vulnerable than she had at the dinner table. She knew her options were limited, and they all involved her ability to calm her husband.

"You're right," she spoke cautiously.

He knew she was trying to placate him. A sneer spread across his features.

"Of course I'm right." He glided over to the tub and resumed his seat on the bath stool. "How're you feeling?"

Ren checked her body for any signs she was hurt. "I'm okay."

He put his hand on her shoulder, and she cringed. He noticed her reaction to his touch, and he narrowed his eyes.

"I don't think you are," he said. "Do you feel dizzy?"

Ren had been concentrating so hard on their argument that she hadn't noticed the tilt of the room. Once she realized her vision was blurring, she panicked.

"What did you do?"

Ren tried to get out of the tub, but her feet and hands kept slipping against the porcelain. She grabbed for the sides, desperate to hoist herself out, but her hands and body wouldn't work in the way she needed.

Kai looked at her with mild amusement. "I didn't think it was going to end this way."

His look of regret and inaction horrified Ren. *What had he done to her?*

She tried to speak, but her words came out gravelly. He nodded as if he understood.

"I thought you were different," he said. "When you devoted your-self to me, you were everything I could have ever wanted. You didn't try to flirt with other men, and you stayed at home. Right where I put you."

Ren was completely incapacitated. She could move her eyes, but she could hardly focus on her husband.

"Murderer," she tried to say, for she knew he meant to kill her, but the sound was barely a whisper that stayed in her mouth.

He looked at her as if he were just noticing her. Broken from the gravity of his thoughts about the relationship they once shared, he spoke.

"Oh, you won't be talking again."

He picked up the card, drenched in wine, and threw it into the tub. She imagined the wine spreading across the water like blood.

"No one will even care you're gone. You don't have any friends, and your parents are content to live their own lives. You were a mistake—just like that baby." He pointed at her stomach. "But that will be corrected soon."

Tears fell from her eyes and rolled down her cheeks. He reached out his hand and caught one on his finger, bringing it to his mouth and licking it.

"We could have been together if you had just tried to save me," he told her. He moved his face inches from hers, his eyes blazing. "WHY DID YOU LEAVE ME?"

Ren couldn't open her mouth to defend herself. Her lips drooped until she was certain she resembled a sad clown.

A smile spread across his face. "That's okay. I found a way to even the score."

He backed away, giving her a pitying look before he nudged her shoulder. She slid, and Kai smiled benignly as her face moved closer to the edge of the water.

"Now you'll know what it feels like to drown while the person you love leaves you to die."

The water was cold, and her nose almost touched the surface. She breathed warm ripples, acutely aware they would be her final breaths. She struggled inside her body, but her limbs were useless. She couldn't move her eyes, but somehow they stayed open, drooping, but giving her a view of her watery doom.

Kai had left the house. She'd heard the garage door open and close even though her ears were ringing.

A thousand thoughts raced through her mind. Most of all, the fear for her unborn child topped the list.

What had she done that was so bad he wanted to kill them? How had the intervention been the final straw?

She wasn't far enough along for a medical team to save the baby if Kai changed his mind and came home, pulling her out of the water. The baby would perish with her, and they'd die watery deaths, the baby in amniotic fluid, and Ren in the tub she'd filled.

Her nose went under the water.

Her hair caused the rest of her head to dip more rapidly. She was still awake and aware as she stared through the murky water at the ceiling.

Panic ripped through her, but she could do nothing. She concentrated on her toes and fingers. If she could just get one of them to move, there was hope that she could escape.

The card floated over her line of vision and *To my loving wife on our anniversary* stared back at her. She was certain Kai would be overjoyed by the irony.

Ren struggled for air, but her mouth stayed closed, and her body didn't move. She was nearing the end, and she was determined to focus on her unborn baby.

She wished she had left the morning after Christmas. She didn't regret her pregnancy, and she would have kept the baby, running anywhere to get away from the monster she had married. *Though, how was she to have known his mind had degraded to the level of a killer? How could she have suspected he resented her enough to murder her?*

As she felt the water enter her throat, Ren longed for the peacefulness of the ocean when she and Kai had gone scuba diving. No matter how much she tried to focus on the water or the baby in her womb, though, panic won out, and she drifted into the arms of death, completely terrified.

When she woke up beside the tub, coughing and vomiting, she was unsure what to do. *Wasn't she dead? She had been alone in the house. Had Kai come back to rescue her?*

A hand touched her shoulder, and she jumped. Kai may have experienced a change of heart and come back to save her, and that was fine, but she wasn't going back to him.

"Rennie."

If she could have turned quickly, she would have seen her hero, but she only managed to shift her body before she fell onto the floor. Her vision blurred as she stared at a sock that had been kicked under the tub on a happier day. Kai's sock.

His hands lifted her, turning her to face him. Gonzo's cheeks were wet with tears, his mascara forming a small ring under his eyes.

"I saw him grab you," he blubbered. "I know I shouldn't have been watching, but I saw him hurt you. I don't know why, but I knew he wasn't finished."

Ren shivered against him. She didn't know if it was because she was scared, cold, or in shock.

He held her around the shoulders as he searched for a towel. She felt fluffy comfort around her body, but the towel wasn't long enough. Even though she was covered, Ren felt exposed. Everything she'd hidden so well, Kai's decline and abusive behavior, was left open for her neighbor.

He'd been watching her house. She didn't know if he'd started that day or if he'd been doing it for a while, but it didn't matter. Gonzo had saved her life.

She felt more comfortable with Gonzo than she had with Kai at the height of their relationship. His tears and the way he held her showed more empathy than she'd ever seen from her husband. Kai went through the motions of compassion well, but Gonzo put them into action.

"How long will he stay gone?"

Ren didn't trust her voice. She shrugged, as she was clueless about what Kai had planned.

She doubted he was going to call the authorities, as he had left the anniversary card and spilled wine in the bathtub. She wondered if the drug he'd used would have shown up in an autopsy.

Gonzo picked her up and carried her to her bedroom. He was very gentle as he dressed her in the outfit she'd chosen before her bath.

After her shirt fell over her shoulders, he rubbed her stomach. "We need to get you to a hospital."

Ren agreed, and Gonzo flew around the room, throwing the things she needed into an overnight bag. He followed her directions, and he located everything but her cell phone.

Ren stared at the floor. "He probably took it with him."

Gonzo put his hand on her arm. "We need to go. I know you may want to take your car, but I think we should take mine."

Ren tried to make it down the steps, but after she almost tripped, Gonzo picked her up again. Even though he was wiry, Gonzo never lost his balance or seemed to run out of energy.

He put her down in a chair at his kitchen table while he warmed the car. He ran upstairs, and when he returned, he rolled a suitcase behind him.

Ren's eyes filled with tears. Gonzo hardly knew her, but he was prepared to stay with her.

He threw their luggage into the car, and Ren made her way to the garage. She thought she heard her name yelled in the wind, and it froze her.

Gonzo heard it, too. "Get in the backseat and lay down. I'll turn off all the lights."

Leaving their neighborhood was agonizing. Gonzo lived in a cul-de-sac behind her, and he had to go past her house to leave the subdivision. As he drove, she counted the streetlights that beamed through the window. She thought she'd be safe after she counted seven of them.

After three lights, Gonzo sucked in his breath. "Stay down," he whispered without moving his lips.

Ren could imagine Kai running around their house looking for her. *What would he do if he knew she was driving past him?*

She counted the seventh streetlight, but she didn't dare move. She trusted Gonzo to let her know when they were safe.

"What's going on?" she whispered.

"Just stay down another minute," he replied.

The lights grew brighter, and the car stopped. Gonzo hurried her out of the car and into the hospital, hardly pausing for the automatic doors to open wide enough to admit them.

The receptionist, a young woman with smooth brown hair, greeted them with a half smile. "How can I help you?"

The question threw off Ren and Gonzo. The way she phrased it suggested that there were many ways she could help, but Ren didn't know where to begin.

Gonzo recovered first. "I think she needs to see a doctor about her baby." He pointed to Ren.

The receptionist started typing. "Are you the father?"

Her eyes were on the screen, so she didn't see the look that passed between Ren and Gonzo. Ren understood that he'd play the part if she needed it, but she wasn't going to use her new friend.

"No, but he's a dear friend," Ren answered.

"What brought you here?"

Ren could feel Gonzo's eyes on her. "I had an accident, and I need to check on the baby."

The receptionist's pink nails clicked against the keys. "What type of accident? Did you fall?"

She felt Gonzo tense up. He'd go along with whatever she said, but it was clear he expected her to implicate her husband.

"Yeah. In the bathtub," she added when she thought about her damp hair.

Ren had visited the emergency room when she'd fallen off a ladder the previous spring. Kai had still been healing, so a neighbor sat with him while she drove to the hospital. Her wrist had been broken, and she'd worn a cast for several weeks.

Due to her last visit, all of Ren's information was on file, so she only had to sign a few waivers. She pressed the electronic keypad with a shaky hand, and Gonzo put his hand on her back. His touch steadied her, and she stood a little straighter.

The receptionist spoke into a speaker attached to her shirt, and a nurse opened the door within a few seconds. A glance around the empty waiting room proved that it was a slow night for injuries in their small town.

Ren and Gonzo were led to the room closest to the door. Ren settled onto the bed, and Gonzo took the chair on the opposite side of the monitors.

The nurse took her vitals and asked for more details. She was trained to read through lies, and she seemed to sense the one Ren gave her. She sat on the bed, placing a plump hand over Ren's fingers.

"It looks like you have a good friend with you," she said.

Ren looked at Gonzo and nodded. "He's been a great friend."

Gonzo made no move to accept the accolades. He continued to stare at the monitor behind Ren's head.

"Are you safe, honey?" the nurse asked.

It was another opportunity for Ren to tell the truth about her horrible experience. She just couldn't seem to get her mouth to move when she decided to speak about it. Aside from her compassion, the nurse looked a lot like Bentley's mother, and she couldn't risk Kai finding out about her plan.

The nurse took her silence for a negative answer. "Can I call someone to help you? They can provide food, shelter, clothes—"

Ren shook her head emphatically. "I can go home."

"Not a chance," Gonzo spoke from his chair.

The nurse patted her arm. "Let's check on the baby first. Then we can talk about what you plan to do."

The nurse strapped a belt around her waist, and a circular piece of metal squeezed against her middle. She guessed it was where the baby was positioned.

A technician came into the room, wheeling a special ultrasound machine behind him. He opened the laptop and started typing.

"Are you the father?"

It was the second time he'd been asked, and Gonzo waited for Ren to answer. She shook her head when the technician looked at her.

"Is that a sensitive subject?"

Ren dropped her eyes. "Yes."

"Fair enough," the technician answered.

Ren had been instructed to undress below the waist, and since Gonzo had put her clothes on, she saw no reason to ask him to leave. She prepared for the wand to be inserted, and a picture of her uterus lit up the screen.

The technician wasn't forthcoming with the information. He explained that the doctor would speak to them about the results.

Another nurse took Ren's blood while they waited for the doctor. Gonzo flipped out his phone and typed furiously until he noticed Ren looking at him.

"It's the guy I was with earlier," he explained, showing her a screen she couldn't read. "I told him I was busy, but he thinks I'm just avoiding him."

Ren laughed dryly. "He'd probably leave you alone if he knew what you were doing."

Gonzo chuckled. "No, he'd try to talk me into adopting your baby and raising it as our own."

Ren stared at the heartbeat on the baby's monitor. "I'd let you."

Gonzo leaned up in his chair and took her hand. "Don't you want your baby?"

A tear traced a track down her cheek and landed on her growing belly. "I want the baby to have a good home. I don't have a good home."

"But it can be," he urged. "Just leave him, and you'll be able to raise the baby—"

"He'll take the baby," Ren told him and burst into tears. "He's already told me he'd take him."

"After he tried to drown you?" Gonzo shot up out of his seat. "No judge in his right mind would—"

"He'll find a way," Ren choked out.

Gonzo sat back down, but his legs moved so fast he could almost have run in his seat. "He's brainwashed you. It's the mark of a true narcissist. Maybe even a psychopath."

Ren didn't want to argue with Gonzo about the changes her husband had experienced over the past year. She thought her neighbor had seen the difference in his habits.

"How long have you been watching the house?" she asked.

The doctor chose that moment to knock. She told Ren that the baby was okay, but they wanted to observe her overnight. Ren went to sleep in the same room, and when she woke up, Gonzo's head was on the bed and their fingers were intertwined.

Ren marveled at how easily she'd formed a connection with Gonzo. She'd spent years in near reclusion, but Gonzo had helped her more in one day than most of her friends had helped her during her life. Ren let her guard down and decided to be as open with him as she had wanted to be with her husband.

He stirred and lifted his head. "I've never woken up beside a woman before."

She smiled at his joke. "I think there's some coffee in the nurses' station."

He got up to get a cup. As he rose, the door opened, and the nurse who had admitted Ren hurried into the room. She glided straight to Ren's bed and took her hand.

"Honey, I'm so sorry."

Ren looked from Gonzo to the nurse. "Is something wrong with the baby?"

A knock echoed against the walls, causing Ren to jump. Another nurse entered the room with two officers.

The officers held their hats in their hands. Ren knew why they were there before they spoke.

"I told Kia you were here," the nurse admitted. Ren had been right. She was Bentley's mother. "The police called Bentley this morning after they found—"

One officer gently nudged the nurse. She moved out of the room, where a woman stood sternly. The woman was there for the nurse, and she led her away.

Ren quietly absorbed the information the officers gave her. Details were limited, but an accident had been reported.

Kai had been found in the lake, and he was dead.

CHAPTER 37

R en stayed in silence for some time. It was probably only minutes, but her mind needed peace. She would never be ready to
resurface, but her tank of oxygen would run out soon, so she had to
go back into the world.

She was proud. She had reclaimed a part of herself that Kai had
tried to take away. She could go back into the water without fear, and
it empowered her. Tears threatened, but she pushed them away. She
finally felt free.

Then it bumped her.

Ren didn't know what type of fish populated the water hole, and
she scrambled for her light. Her underwater flashlight switched on
and cast a beam of light straight in front of her.

That's when her peace shattered.

She flicked her light in one direction and another, but the grisly
scenes were the same. No one could hear her screams, but they
echoed in her ears as she stared at the bodies surrounding her.

"She's awake," he said.

Ren felt the world come back to her in a rollercoaster rush of sound. She searched for her last memory, but when it came to her, the shock almost sent her over the edge again.

Jonas's arms were around her before she opened her eyes. She tried to sit up and found herself naked on her couch.

"Hey, there." He pushed a piece of hair behind her ear. "We were worried about you."

We? Ren thought, and then she remembered. Jonas had a split personality disorder.

Carefully, she moved into a sitting position. She could do nothing about her wide-eyed stare, and he picked up on it immediately.

Jonas looked behind them before whispering in her ear. "I didn't kill them."

Ren tried to keep her features unreadable and remained silent. Any wrong move could set him off.

She quickly evaluated what she knew about Jonas. He was kind and sweet, but even if his alter ego had killed the people she saw floating in the water, Jonas had known about them.

"I have to go," he told her. "My brother will be here to watch over you."

He handed clothes to her, and she grabbed her panties first. She couldn't slip them on quickly enough, and she was shaking from what she assumed was shock.

"I pulled you out." He announced it proudly, and an innocent smile touched his lips.

"T-Thank you," Ren responded, as she knew he was waiting for her acknowledgment.

"You need someone to look after you," he replied, placing the shirt over her head. "You're always getting yourself into trouble."

She wished she were dreaming. She hoped the shirt that came between her sight of him would change the scene as she pushed her head into it. Perhaps on the other side, she'd be home and not in the presence of a murderer.

Once her clothes were on, he looked her over, inspecting his handiwork. "You can't leave now."

Ren was aware she knew too much for Jonas to allow her to leave peacefully. She'd have to make him think she wanted to be with him so he would spare her life. At some point, his attention would waver, and then she could run for help.

She brought her hand to his face. She took in her trembling fingers and forced her face into what she hoped was a lover's expression.

"I don't want you to leave me."

He checked her for sincerity and nodded. "I know, but I have to secure one of the members. You disrupted the collection, and I have to tie her back to her block."

Ren thought about the bodies nudging her in the quiet water hole. Jonas had said it was deep, but it couldn't have been more than twenty-five feet to the bottom. He told her he tied the victims' feet to a rope attached to a concrete block, and it held them in place as they swayed in the water.

Bodies that were in varying degrees of decomposition had moved in the water. Skeletal fingers had reached for her as if they had been asking her to help pull them out of their watery grave.

"I love you." He waited for her response, and Ren lied to him as quickly as her mouth would move.

"I love you, too."

Satisfied with her answer, Jonas patted her hands and lifted off the couch. "Don't try to leave. Riley will stop you, and he's not as nice as me." He leaned over, whispering so softly she could hardly hear him. "He kills them, but he has me arrange them."

Ren shuddered, but she tried to cover it as a shiver. She hugged herself tightly.

Jonas spread the afghan on the back of the couch over her shoulders. "You'll be fine until I get back. Just don't make him mad."

He tromped to the basement door and opened it before shouting down. "I'm going to take care of that thing you want me to do. I'll be back soon." He glanced at Ren before he added, "Remember your promise."

He didn't wait for a response, as a dark basement couldn't provide him with one, and he shut the door hard as he left. Ren was left alone, and she flew into action.

In case he was watching from the windows, she crept slowly across the floor. Her phone was still on the counter. Either it was left there due to Jonas's extreme oversight or because he had disabled it.

Ren was thankful the low evening sun kept the backlight on her phone from illuminating the room. She typed in her passcode and dialed emergency services. The woman on the other end of the line asked her for a city and county, but she could only offer Watauga

Lake and her address. She'd never learned the county, and she couldn't pin down the zip code.

A sound in the basement startled her, and she dropped the phone. Her thumb hit the screen as she lifted it, and the call disconnected. It occurred to Ren that she hadn't relayed her emergency, and no one would know how she died if she suddenly disappeared.

She typed two quick sentences to Gonzo. No matter how angry he was at her, he'd make sure her words were heard.

Her finger hovered over the send button when she heard the feet on the steps. She dropped the phone again and hoped the message was on its way to her friend.

The basement door opened, and Jonas smirked at her. "Now, just what are you doing?"

He spotted the phone, and Ren made no move to grab it. He charged over and broke it with a snap, throwing it at her midsection.

"No one can help you. Even if they came here, you'd be long gone before they could get to you."

Ren's mind raced. She had to acknowledge Jonas's other personality as completely separate from him, so she could establish a deeper connection with Jonas when he stepped back into the situation.

"Jonas wanted you to remember your promise."

He kicked her in the ribs and her breath shot out. Red hot pain traced its way across her body, from her hip to her shoulder. She was thankful Jonas had changed into his sneakers when he assumed his other personality, as the tip of his boot would have caused more damage.

He pulled her head up by her hair. "Jonas isn't here."

He tilted his head, and Ren noticed the part he'd made at the side of his head. There was another difference, too, but the pain was so fresh that she couldn't absorb his changes.

He got up and grabbed her arms, forcing her to stand. If she hadn't kept up with him, he would have dragged Ren down as her body slapped the basement steps.

He moved around the concrete partition as he held her wrists and revealed another person behind them. The woman's shimmering hair was matted and stuck up in angles, and her eyeliner had traced paths down her cheeks.

"The more the merrier!" he announced, slinging her next to Becky.

Instinctively, Ren grabbed the woman for solidarity against their attacker, but Jonas laughed. "It'll be fun to tear the two of you apart." He chuckled. "Two peas in a pod, aren't ya? You think you can go bed-hoppin' around, and no one will know the difference."

He came within inches of Ren's nose and tapped the skin next to his eye. "I see you. I know what you do. Kai was too weak to finish the job, but I'm not."

The look on her face told him she hadn't expected him to know about that incident in her life. Up to that point, she'd thought she and Gonzo were the only living people who knew her husband had tried to drown her.

Ren's mind matched puzzle pieces together that had never fit until that moment. "You killed him."

Jonas's palms went up. "It was an accident. There was nothing I could do."

It was obviously a lie, as he smiled when he said it. Kai had been found attached to a log, but Ren wondered if his body had been moved after his death. *Had his ankles been tied to a concrete block in the same way as the bodies Ren had witnessed floating in the water hole?*

"Why?"

Her question was automatic, and the only reason she could imagine was that Kai had found a woman in the basement before Jonas could get rid of her. He hadn't expected Kai to return so soon, and maybe her husband had stumbled on the scene after he ran from attempting to murder his wife and unborn child.

Undoubtedly, Jonas had done her a favor, but she had felt more closure when she believed Kai's death had been an accident. To her, it was like the universe had rewarded her pleas for justice in the form of her husband's miscalculations as he swam past a large log in the lake.

"I told you," Jonas answered. "He was weak."

There was a part of Ren that still wanted to defend her husband, but she had broken through the perfect picture she'd painted of Kai and accepted him as a man who needed help but was too ashamed to seek it. Still, she wanted to know why Kai was easily expendable.

"Did you kill him because he discovered your little secret?" She spat the words, hoping to goad him into telling her the truth.

He narrowed his eyes before his expression cleared. It was such a drastic change that she thought he might be switching back to his more compassionate personality.

Beside her, Becky squirmed in her bonds, knocking the handcuffs against the pipe to which she was cuffed. She screamed into the cloth tied around her mouth. Blood had soaked through most of the area around her mouth, giving her a clown-like appearance.

"Jonas?" Ren tried. She started to stand, but kept her body low, so to appear like less of a threat.

Jonas snarled and pushed her down. "You have no idea what's going on, do you?"

He laughed and turned around in a circle. Apparently, Becky had seen the behavior before, and she struggled harder against her bonds. The scuffing of cuffs against the pipe reminded Ren of the tapping sound she'd heard when she first arrived at the lake house, and her stomach turned.

At that point, Jonas hadn't taken Becky. *Who had been making noises in the basement?*

She thought it had been a wild animal. *What if Jonas had buried a human body instead of an animal in the woods between their houses?* No wonder he didn't want her to go anywhere near the grave he'd dug for the "wild animal" he'd buried there.

Jonas picked up a rope and wrapped it around her wrists. She stumbled backward, and he shoved her against Becky as he tied the rope to the pipe.

Ren struggled against him, but he was much stronger than her. He pressed his mouth to her lips, and she tasted salt and caramel. Trying to bite his lip, she moved her mouth against his, but he was too quick for her.

"You still remember our time together, don't you?" He wiped his mouth. "It was so much better than anything my brother could do."

Ren noticed the bruises on Becky's wrists and realized she had been violated while she was held prisoner. Her heart went out to the woman as she imagined she had been sleeping or going peacefully through her daily routine as Becky endured any number of tortures at Jonas's hands.

Ren's eyes widened as she took in the green shirt and tan shorts she'd worn on her first date with Jonas. She hadn't even noticed they were gone. Becky had been abducted on the lake, so she had probably been in a swimsuit. Jonas had gotten clothes for his victim out of Ren's closet. Bile climbed her throat when she thought about other missing clothes that may have been unnoticed.

She tried to reawaken the image of the bodies floating in the water hole. *Had any of them been dressed in her clothes?*

Jonas stood back and admired the knots he'd tied in the rope. "It's not the quality of a pair of handcuffs, but it's as good as the ones my momma made."

Ren remembered the abuse Jonas had discussed with her. "And where is she now? What did you do with her?"

His grin widened. "She was the first in my collection." He caressed Ren's cheek, and she jerked away.

"Not everybody gets to keep momma company in the dark." He kicked Becky. "Some of them go in the woods, but there are others" —he put his hand on Ren's breast— "that will go where I can see them whenever I want."

Ren squirmed and wiggled away, but he backed her into the concrete wall. She pressed the side of her face into it, getting herself as far away from him as possible.

"I'm going to enjoy this," he said, dragging his tongue from her jaw to her temple.

Just as soon as he started, he stopped, glancing at the floor above them. Without a word, he stuffed a piece of cloth into Ren's mouth, fixing it in place with a strip of duct tape, and bolted to the stairs.

Ren realized too late that she should have screamed. She hadn't known Jonas had sensed another person in the house.

Ren and Becky worked on trying to free her bonds. Becky twisted her hands to unhook a knot, but her fingers fell short of it.

Jonas ran down the steps and winced when he saw Ren. He pulled her up, stripping off the tape with a swift pull. Ren doubled over from the sharp pain, but the skin around her mouth was only a dull throb compared to her ribs.

"You aren't supposed to be down here." Jonas unbound her.

Ren was ready to plead with Jonas's milder self. "He's going to kill me and add me to his collection."

Jonas shook his head. "We agreed. You're mine."

He pulled her in the direction of the stairs. Ren pushed her feet down, stopping them.

"What about Becky?"

Jonas cast an unsympathetic look at the broken woman. "She's his. He gets to keep her."

The finality of his tone and everything it implied shocked Ren. It was as if the brothers were amicably dividing toys.

Ren wasn't surprised when Jonas led her out the door. Ren glimpsed her car, and she tried to run for it, but Jonas tripped her with his boot. She landed hard on the ground, tree roots slamming into her hip and cheek.

Jonas pulled her up and carried her down the path. Ren struggled, kicking and screaming, but she only upset the birds on the otherwise quiet forest path.

He opened his door and kicked it closed. Nothing moved in the house as he carried her up a flight of stairs.

Ren had little time to take in her surroundings, but she smelled the same pine scent that lingered on Jonas like a light cologne. He stopped at the first room next to the stairs, and Ren spotted a family portrait. The mother, father, and two sons looked almost exactly alike, with dark hair, green eyes, and grim expressions. The only difference between the sons was a slight difference in height and their hair. The older boy parted it down one side.

Ren stared at Riley in the picture, and something nudged her mind, but the thought was quickly abandoned as Jonas carried her into his room. The smell was the first thing that hit her. She coughed and gagged until Jonas handed her a paper bag.

"You'll get used to it," he told her. "Sometimes the smell gets me, and I have to use one of the bags, but I try not to let her see me do it."

He pointed to the corner of the room, and Ren's eyes followed. When she saw the emancipated, decomposed body of a young woman slumped on the floor, she screamed.

Her next thoughts were drowned in shadows.

CHAPTER 38

Ren woke in the darkness. At first, she thought she was in her bed, but the undertones of the smell in the room were almost too much for her to bear. Despite her attempts to remain quiet and assess her situation, she started coughing.

The sound woke Jonas, who had laid down beside her. He held one of her hands firmly in his fist, and when he moved, it sent tingles down her arm. She cried out as the blood refilled her arm, stinging her in its urgentness.

Jonas rubbed his eyes. "What's wrong, sweetheart?"

Ren lunged across him, but she only succeeded in hanging over him. He had bound her feet to the bedposts.

Jonas pulled her back beside him, rubbing her hair. "You'll get used to it. I used to leave every morning to tend to Colette, but now that you're here, I won't have to do that anymore."

He hugged her tightly, as Ren stifled a scream. "I know it's a little strange to have her watch us, but she's not been able to sleep in bed with me since you've been here." He kissed the top of her nose. "So, I haven't really cheated on you."

Ren realized what Jonas meant to do to her. She wondered if it was better to be in his bedroom, slowly starving as he loved her to death, or in the basement with his other personality. The "Riley" part of Jonas may beat her to death, but she thought she might die a little quicker at his hands.

Jonas kissed her and edged up her shirt. She lay on the bed, completely unresponsive.

She needed to find a way to get back to Becky, and she wasn't helping either of them by letting Jonas do whatever he wanted to her. She had to take charge of the situation somehow, but she didn't know what to do.

Jonas misread her disinterest in his advances. "Don't worry about Colette. She's not able to be intimate with me anymore." He scrunched up his nose, and the moonlight made his face look almost gruesome. "I don't think she ever really got over Riley. When I brought her here, she wasn't as" —he searched for the word— "fun as before she slept with him."

Probably because you forced her to stay here and raped her, Ren thought.

If she was able to see his face, then there was enough light for Jonas to read her expressions, so she tried to relax her features. Another coughing fit took over, and she threw up some bile into another bag.

After she recovered, Jonas pounced on her again. He pulled at her clothes, and Ren's mind raced for a way to get away from him.

"I want Riley," she blurted. "I liked it better with him."

Jonas's face was unreadable. "If Colette is bothering you, I can take her to the woods with Delaney, Jessica, and Cristy. I just want her to see us together one time, so she knows what she's missing."

Ren panicked. She'd found Augusta's friend, and even though she'd assumed Jonas had something to do with her disappearance when she saw the bodies in the water, it was difficult to hear the confirmation.

Jonas stroked her face. "Don't worry. I know they'll still be close by, but I'm done with them."

His promise meant nothing to Ren, and she fumbled for a way to get out of his room. "I mean it, Jonas. I want Riley."

The hand that had been gently holding her shoulder tightened. The pain was fast and fierce, and Ren cried out.

"I think you saw what happened to the last—"

"I don't care," Ren spoke out, surprised by her firmness. "Riley will come to get me if you don't let me go. He told me he wanted me."

Jonas put his hand around her neck. The pressure wasn't enough to choke her, but he wanted to show Ren he had the power to end her life.

"That's a lie," he growled.

"I want Riley," Ren repeated.

The hand around her neck tightened, making her lose her breath. Ren grabbed his arm with both hands, clawing and pulling, but she was unable to move him.

Jonas released her and fell back on his pillow. With another quick movement that caused Ren to jump, he hastily untied her ankles.

"Go to him."

Ren could hardly believe her luck. Jonas had untied her and was giving her the freedom to move between the houses. She couldn't run to her car, as she had no idea where to find her keys, but she could make her way to the nearest neighbor's house. If the person closest to her answered their door right away, she could be in touch with the authorities in less than fifteen minutes.

"Go!" Jonas commanded.

Ren didn't need another invitation. She bolted out of the bedroom and stumbled down the steps. Jonas had locked the front door, but Ren opened it easily.

Outside, she calculated the right direction in which to run. Jonas's house was at the end of the road, so she'd have to go down the path and past her car to get to the nearest neighbor. She hoped Mrs. Ruble was awake and open to the idea of letting a frantic woman into her house in the middle of the night.

She sprinted down the path, only tripping once on a tree root. Blue lights were flashing, but they were across the dock, possibly at Becky's house. She wondered if it would be quicker to run there and decided against it. She'd seek safety, and they could come to her.

Regaining her footing was easy, and she barreled along until she saw her car. One of the tires had been deflated, and as she watched, Jonas revealed himself from the other side of her vehicle. He was playing the part of Riley, and Ren could only stare and wonder how he'd beaten her down the path.

"You came back," he observed, a cruel smile stretching across his face. "Now we can have some fun."

How had Jonas gotten ahead of her?

Ren assumed there was a shorter way back to the house than the path. She'd stopped for a moment to assess the distance between Jonas's and Mrs. Ruble's houses, and there were a few lost moments when she debated swimming to Becky's dock. It must have been enough time for him to throw on a pair of tennis shoes and gain the advantage.

Ren fought with all the strength she had left, but she still found herself in the basement of the lake house. Jonas shoved her into Becky.

He grabbed her hands, but instead of tying them with the rope, he handcuffed her to the pipe. Ren wondered if Jonas had found another pair until she realized that Becky hadn't moved when Ren crashed into her. A quick look confirmed her suspicions.

Becky's body lay at an unnatural angle, and her eyes bulged. The clothes in which she'd been dressed were thrown into a pile beside her head. Ren couldn't study her beyond the initial look, as Jonas demanded her attention.

"Seeing you here gave her hope," he said, his eyes narrowing. "I had to end that."

Now that she was inches away from the monster and whatever he had planned for her, Ren was out of ideas. She tried to keep him talking, in hopes she could figure out something before he attacked her again.

"Why do you kill women?"

Jonas chucked. "Why wouldn't I?" He dusted off his jeans as he stood. "Women control everything, from sex to the way people around them think, so why wouldn't I want to kill them?" He dove at Ren, pressing their noses together. "Seeing the light go out in their eyes is like watching a leader fall in battle. I end their influence on the world, one at a time."

Ren's throat was dry, but she spoke around it. "But why keep them?"

He moved away and shrugged. "Battle trophies?" He laughed. "Why do I need a reason? Kai didn't have a reason."

The shock was plain on her face. Jonas took it in like he was savoring a fine wine before swallowing it.

"You didn't figure it out?"

Ren couldn't move as Jonas sat in front of her on his knees. He traced her jaw with his fingers and pinched her neck. The motion got the reaction he wanted.

"Yes, my diluted little slut. While you were at home, sleeping with your neighbor, Kai was here, helping me add to my collection."

Ren couldn't find the words to defend herself. Gonzo was gay, and she hardly saw him before the day her husband had tried to kill her. She hadn't been promiscuous before she'd met Kai, and she'd been faithful throughout their marriage.

"Oh, this is fun," he went on, and excitement lit up his cheeks, showcasing the dimple by his chin.

Jonas danced around the room like a child, clapping his hands. He settled back in front of her, mocking her with a compassionate smile.

"Honey, your husband slept with over half the women who vacationed at this lake." He checked her response, and when he assessed that she was speechless, he went on. "Over the years, he only added a handful to the collection, but since he killed my momma—"

Ren finally found her voice. "What?"

She thought she'd been her husband's first intended victim. Then, moments ago, she'd imagined he'd helped Jonas with his terrible plans. She'd been able to digest that he'd killed women when he'd visited the lake after his accident, but the idea that he had killed someone *before* they almost died in the car wreck was almost too much for her to process. She had lived with a murderer, even before his mind had started to change.

Jonas clapped his hands. "Oh! I love story time."

CHAPTER 39

He sat down in front of her and crossed his legs. He stared at her pointedly until she did the same.

"Once upon a time, there was an evil witch who lived on the lake. She stayed there with a troll and their two sons."

Ren held his eyes, afraid to move. Maybe if she listened to his crazy fairytale, she could find something in it to help her.

"The troll hardly ever paid attention to the witch or their sons, but he took them to a magical water hole that kept the evil out of the world.

"When the troll was away, the witch was mean to her boys, locking them in the dungeon for hours while she did unspeakable things with the neighbors. The boys could hear her through the ventilation system, and when she was at the height of her passion, they banged on the pipes and yelled out the windows for help.

"When she heard them shouting, the witch would wait until her lovers left, and she would rampage through the house. She'd grab one boy and beat him while the other begged for her to stop."

Despite his evil nature, Ren found tears in her eyes. At that point, Jonas and Riley had been young boys, and Jonas hadn't turned into the monster before her.

"The witch broke one boy's arm, and a couple of ribs on the other one, but the scars she left were deeper than the ones on the surface. The troll would free the boys from their prison, but the witch would charm him with her beauty and put a spell on him. She'd make a potion and pass it off as wine. After the troll drank it, he'd forget her crimes."

If someone had told Ren that Jonas could outdo her in his storytelling abilities, she would have laughed in their face. However, it wasn't really Jonas who had concocted the tale based on his horrible experiences. It was the alter ego that had risen to the surface after years of abuse.

"One day, the boys didn't go easily into the dungeon when one of her lovers called. They stood their ground together, convinced they could overpower her.

"The witch took a knife and cut the younger boy's arm. She threatened to stab them if they didn't let her lock them away. The boys complied, and they stayed in the darkness for hours."

Jonas emotionally recounted the height of his abuse. Once he'd blinked away glassy eyes, he continued.

"The younger boy's arm didn't stop bleeding. She'd cut him near his wrist, and even though the knife hadn't seemed to go very deep, the wound wouldn't stop bleeding. The older boy took off his shirt and applied pressure to the wound, but no matter how much pressure the older brother held onto it, the place where she had cut him almost gushed.

"The older brother screamed for help. He yelled until he was hoarse, but no one rescued them.

"The boys had made a friend who lived in the house next to them, but it was still a good distance away. At times, the neighbor would take a walk in the woods, but it was usually in the early morning.

"That day, he'd had an early appointment, so he hadn't been able to take his walk until the afternoon. The neighbor heard the boys yelling from their prison and sought to free them. He broke a window, but it was too small for the boys to fit through.

"The boys pleaded with him not to call emergency services, as when they'd depended on them before, the witch had made their lives harder. Instead, the neighbor brought them an emergency kit, and they plotted a way to end the witch's evil reign."

Her husband had been the neighbor in the story, and she couldn't say she would have been unaffected by the boys' plight. They were abused, and they had tried to tell everyone who witnessed the signs, but no one would get them away from their mother.

"The neighbor was crafty, and he found a way into the witch's bed," Jonas went on. "When he was at the door, the boys went willingly into the basement, knowing their plan was working.

"The witch trusted the neighbor, so when he suggested they share a bottle of wine, she fetched the glasses. Soon, she was unable to move, stuck in the same wakeful sleep that she'd put the troll in for years.

"The boys carried her to the magical well, and after tying a cinder block to her ankle, tossed her into it. They counted the minutes, and after ten of them had passed, they knew she was dead. Just to be sure, the neighbor dove and found her lifeless body in the water."

Jonas jumped up and clapped his hands together. "The boys were free!" He paced the length of the room, bouncing on his heels. "They told the stupid troll the witch left with one of her lovers, and he believed them." He put a finger on his chin. "Or he knew, and he didn't care."

Jonas's face darkened, and his hands curled into fists. "But then the troll brought other witches around, and the boys knew it would only be a matter of time before they were back in the dungeon."

"You killed them," Ren said. She didn't know why she felt so brave, but Jonas's anger was focused elsewhere, so she took advantage of it.

"I killed the ones who wanted to stay around," he emphasized. "*I* took the light from their eyes."

He scoffed. "It turns out older women fall for young boys all the time, and nobody misses them."

"Not every woman feels that way."

He rolled his eyes. "I'd just turned eighteen, and I was good at getting any woman I wanted. My brother focused on the young girls, but I put my attention on the older women. All I had to do was give them a little attention, and they'd do anything I asked."

He picked up a knife from a table littered with tools. Ren understood the knife and the hammer, but other objects, like the wrench, made her wonder about their uses in his torture sessions. Rust-colored stains caught the light as he moved the knife from side to side.

"I could cut out your heart, you know." He spoke casually, as if he were informing her about a shared interest. "Kai was supposed to do that to you, but he backed out."

"I'm sure it wasn't the first time he did something you didn't like."

Jonas was on her as fast as lightning, touching the knife to the skin of her throat. Blood trickled onto her chest.

"You're right about that." He pulled away just enough to absorb her fear. He sucked it in, almost tasting it. "He wasn't supposed to marry you." He forced a dry laugh. "You were supposed to be part of the collection, but he *fell in love*." He put air quotes around the last words, attempting to mock her husband's voice.

Ren had to keep him talking. She had a feeling when the conversation stopped, Jonas would find ways to entertain himself, and she wouldn't like any of his ideas.

"Why didn't he just kill me after our first fight?" she asked. "If you don't think he really loved me, why wouldn't he have put me in your collection a long time ago?"

Jonas didn't answer her question. "It's not my collection. It belongs to me, Jonas, Kai, and my dad." He held up a finger each time he named a person.

"Your dad?" she questioned.

A smile spread across his face. "He'd already lived with one witch; he wasn't going to suffer through any more of them."

"But I thought *you* killed them?"

He nodded along with her words. "I got one or two. He got the rest."

"Are you telling me that no one missed any of the women?"

He chuckled and threw her a look from the side. "No one misses a whore."

He went to the back of the room, where a loaf of bread sat on the table. He tore off a chunk of bread and offered her a piece. She shook her head.

At least this side of him feeds his victims, she thought.

He chewed a bite of bread and talked around it. "I don't think you realize what Mother did to our family. She drugged her husband, kept us away from most people, and locked us in a dark basement for most of our childhoods."

Jonas watched a tear fall from her eye. "It's no worse than what you did to your family."

"I did nothing to my family," Ren seethed.

He laughed in her face so hard that pieces of bread flew out of his mouth and stuck to her cheek. "You keep telling yourself that."

Ren wiped her cheek with her shoulder. "How did I do anything? My husband tried to kill me."

"You weren't the only one he was trying to get rid of."

Ren's mouth went dry. Kai had told Jonas about her pregnancy.

"Did you think you could just get rid of the kid and no one would know?"

She said nothing. Gonzo should have been the only living person who knew about her child.

"Anyway," he went on, "You left your husband in a car to die, and then you got pregnant by your neighbor."

"It was Kai's baby!" she shot back.

"He wouldn't do that," Jonas said, shaking his head. "He said there was no way the baby was his."

Ren felt like cold water had been splashed on her. She had gotten pregnant after only one time without protection. *Had Kai forgotten their Christmas promise?*

"Do you finally see why he'd want to kill you?"

Ren was trying to process so much that she felt like her head would explode. She had loved a man who had tried to kill her and their unborn child, but even if he believed the baby belonged to someone else, he should have simply divorced her.

"I'm not a bad person," Ren said, but her head dropped.

It was all Jonas needed to pounce on her again. This time she let him, hoping he'd lose interest if she didn't fight him. Her idea worked, as he backed away, slapping her lightly on her cheek.

"I'll be back," he promised. "I have plenty of time to break your spirit."

He lifted off her body and walked around the partition, leaving her with Becky's body. She stared at the woman, noting the fingerprints on her swollen neck.

She didn't realize she was crying until she spoke. "I'm sorry I couldn't help you."

The door shut upstairs, and she waited until she thought Jonas was far enough away before she started screaming for help. The reality of the situation was clear. Jonas wouldn't have left without gagging her if he thought someone was close enough to hear her. She was alone.

She stopped trying to yell and focused on the handcuffs. As she moved them across the pipe, they reminded her of the sounds she'd heard. *Had another woman been trying to free herself as Ren listened upstairs?* The thought made her sick.

She'd drifted into a trance-like state that wasn't anything like dreaming when she heard it. A soft scraping sounded at the door. Ren braced herself as footsteps descended.

"Rennie!" a voice whisper-shouted.

Relief flooded her body. "Gonzo!"

He whipped around the wall and into the room, stumbling backward at the sight of her.

"Oh my—" His bottom lip shook. "Who did this to you?"

Without waiting for her answer, he started trying to unfasten her handcuffs. As he looked around for a key, his eyes landed on Becky, and he screamed.

His hand went to his heart, and he stumbled backward. He stayed locked on the dead body, his breaths short and strained.

Ren sat up, fell back once, and approached her friend cautiously. "Gonzo, we need to get out of here. Did you bring your car?"

He nodded. "It's parked beside yours."

He needed time to process the scene, but they had to hurry. If Jonas saw his car parked next to Ren's, they'd both be killed.

Ren grabbed Gonzo's chin and forced him to look at her. "What happened to Becky was terrible, but we need to go now."

He nodded, but his eyes kept darting back to the corpse on the basement floor. "Did you see her—"

Ren cut him off by raising her hand. She thought she'd heard a scrape in the kitchen, like someone had moved a chair.

She dragged Gonzo to the steps and looked up. Jonas was standing at the top of the stairs with a gun in his hand.

Chapter 40

Gonzo pulled Ren's arm and tried to lead her away, but Ren stayed in place. If she lost sight of the monster, he would have the advantage, and she wasn't giving him any more than he'd already claimed.

"I've only killed one other man," Jonas said, taking a step down. "But I don't mind a little more of a challenge."

Ren had to think of him as Jonas. She'd left the milder-mannered personality at his family's house, but she hoped Jonas would resurface. Even though he was upset with her for choosing his brother over him, Jonas might not kill her.

When he was halfway down the steps, Ren threw the handcuffs at him. They hit him just above the eye, and Jonas held his face.

"You little—"

Ren ran. She grabbed Gonzo by the hand and pulled him to the nearest window. He hoisted her up to it, but the glass wouldn't move. Large nails poked out from the bottom, sealing it shut.

"You learned from my story," Jonas acknowledged from behind them. A large, purple bruise was forming over his eyebrow. "I had Jonas nail them shut. I didn't want to risk anyone escaping."

Gonzo stared at Ren, horrified, and completely in the dark. He needed a little context, but Ren didn't know if she could tell him about Jonas's split personality disorder while pretending the person in front of her was a separate entity.

"So, this is Gonzo," Jonas mused. "Is he the one Kai saw walking out of his house with a bottle of wine?"

Ren thought back to the day Gonzo had helped her unload the supplies for Kai's intervention. *Had Kai been watching her?* If so, he must have thought she'd slept with Gonzo when he staggered out with a bottle of wine.

"He's gay," she said flatly.

Jonas circled closer to Gonzo, sizing him up. "Are you sure he—"

"I'm sure!" she yelled. She was pretty certain Jonas didn't plan to kill her quickly, so she could afford a few harsh words.

"Whose baby was it then?" Jonas demanded.

"She was my husband's baby!" Ren shouted, coming completely undone. "He got me pregnant on Christmas day and forgot about it. Is that what you want to hear?"

Jonas chuckled. "He forgot about a lot of things, didn't he?"

Ren stood still, facing down the man in her path. She wondered if she could knock him over, allowing Gonzo the opportunity to run for help.

"What happened to the baby?" Jonas asked, moving closer to her. "You weren't cut out for mothering, were you?"

Ren's eyes filled with tears. She blinked most of them away, but one fell out of each eye.

"You don't deserve to know."

He was on her faster than she could blink, lifting her up by the shirt. "You have a choice. You can answer me and do whatever I say, or I can shoot your friend."

"You can only shoot me once," Gonzo spoke bravely. "Ren doesn't have to do anything you say."

Jonas scratched his temple with the gun. "That's true."

The force of his head crashing against hers rattled her skull. Ren's vision doubled before she was able to focus.

Gonzo's palms shot up. "Stop! I'll be quiet!"

He wrung his hands and stayed in place, even though he could have run. There was a good chance he could have made it to the steps before Jonas would have angled himself to shoot at him, but Gonzo didn't move.

Jonas put Ren over his shoulder and carried her back to where Becky lay. Ren purposefully didn't look at her, and she held her hand out dreamily when Jonas slapped the handcuff over it. There was no use fighting him when Gonzo's life was at stake. Jonas wrapped the metal between the cuffs around the pipe, putting it between the pipe and the wall, and placed the other cuff on Gonzo.

Why didn't her friend get away! she thought. He may not have wanted to leave her, but he could have run for help and saved himself.

Ren had pulled Gonzo into a lethal situation, and she regretted it. Part of her had to have known he would do anything to save her, even if it meant giving up his life.

She may not murder him, but she had killed Gonzo as soon as she'd called and messaged for his help. She had to think of a way to get them both out alive.

Ren thought her cuff felt loose, and she tried to signal it to Gonzo when Jonas turned his back. Gonzo nodded his understanding, eyeing Jonas like a wild animal.

"Now," Jonas said, settling in front of them. "I'm ready to have some fun. Who's ready to go first?"

He looked from Ren to Gonzo, but neither of them spoke.

"No takers?" he said. "Okay, then. Let's start with you."

He pointed to Gonzo. "Does anyone know you're here?"

Gonzo hesitated just long enough, and Jonas realized his next words were lies. Before he spoke, Jonas delivered a swinging jab to Ren's cheek. Ren cried out, and Gonzo screamed.

"Okay, okay! My boyfriend knows I'm here."

Jonas's mouth formed a grim line. "I need his name and address."

Gonzo looked at Ren before he gave him the requested information. Ren had hoped he'd give out a fake address, but from what she could tell, Gonzo had sold out his boyfriend for Ren's safety. It was too bad it couldn't last.

"How did you know to come here?" Jonas asked him.

Ren didn't look at her friend. Her cheek stung, and she didn't want the abuse she'd received to affect his answer.

"I should have come sooner," he replied, and Ren knew he was talking to her more than answering Jonas's question. "Ren needed me, but I was so mad at her for screwing around with you I left, and when she called Blane, I made him lie and say he hadn't seen me."

"Ren," Jonas said, expecting her to look up. Instead, she focused on a chip in her nail polish, wishing to go back to when she'd last painted them.

"What happened to the kid?"

He went straight to the most sensitive issue. Ren had seen the way he'd handled Gonzo when he'd lied, so she didn't want to chance her friend's life. She reasoned that the information wouldn't go beyond the three of them, as when Jonas killed Gonzo and her, he wouldn't have anyone outside of the bodies in his "collection" with whom to share her deepest secret.

Gonzo brought their cuffed hands together, giving her the strength to speak. She took a shaky breath, a plan forming in her mind.

"She was born four weeks early," she told him. "I'd thought I was having a boy, but the moment they put her in my arms, I realized how silly I was to have thought it. She had Kai's eyes and nose, but her hair was the same color as mine. I thought all babies were born with raven black hair, but—"

"Blah, blah, blah," Jonas said, hitting her shin with the side of his hand. "No one wants to hear the sappy—"

"What do you want to know, then?" Ren countered. "I was telling you what happened."

"No, you were telling me about what your baby looked like. I want to know what you did with her."

"She died," Gonzo said, his voice gravelly with emotion. "Ren told you she was born early. She didn't make it."

Jonas's eyes narrowed. "I don't believe you. Why wasn't there an obituary?"

"You don't have to write one," Ren answered. "No one knew about her besides me, except for Kai, Gonzo, and, apparently, you."

Jonas stood up. "Why were you so ashamed of your baby if she was really Kai's? You were married, and it doesn't seem like you told anyone that he tried to kill you."

"I wasn't ashamed of her," Ren blubbered, overcome with the thoughts of her infant daughter. "I was ashamed of myself."

"You should be," Jonas said. "You slept around on your husband, and you didn't deserve him."

"You loved him," Gonzo observed.

The realization broke the calm in the room, and Jonas beat him on the head with the gun. Ren threw herself into the fight, taking many of the blows on her hands and arms.

Jonas backed away, fixing the gun on Gonzo. "I can have any woman I want!"

"Okay," Gonzo said, his mouth streaming with blood. "I won't tell anyone you wanted to screw Kai." Suddenly brave, he spat a tooth on the ground at Jonas's feet. "What's it to me if you slept with the same women Kai slept with, just so you could feel like you had been with him."

Jonas screamed in rage. "Shut up!"

"Then you killed them so Kai couldn't sleep with them again."

Ren had to admit, it made a lot of sense. Jonas's mother had triggered his mental illness into a darker form, but Jonas's suppressed desires caused him to murder the women who were unlucky enough to fall for his dimple and perfect smile.

"Kai's dead!" he yelled at him. "Why would I need to keep him away from any more women?"

Gonzo picked a thread on his shirt. "Maybe you just like the rush, but I think you're getting rid of all his lovers." He motioned to Becky's dead body without looking at her, attempting to prove his point.

Ren hadn't thought about Kai sleeping with Becky. Jonas had mentioned that Kai had slept with over half the women who visited the lake, and Becky had been beautiful.

Jealosy didn't even twinge her heart. She felt a deeper sorrow for Becky, and forgave her for sleeping with her husband.

His frustration and anger mounting, Jonas backed up and snarled. He started to speak and stopped. His reaction was fierce, and Ren didn't anticipate it.

Jonas fired the gun twice as he screamed. The shots rang against the walls, and Ren covered her ears with her free hand.

One bullet hit the sheetrock behind Gonzo, but the other pelted him in the chest. He fell back, and Ren screamed.

CHAPTER 41

Jonas grabbed Ren after unlocking the handcuffs. She kicked and screamed for her friend as Jonas effortlessly carried her away.

He had trouble balancing her up the steps, but knocking her head against the doorframe dazed her enough for him to get her into her bedroom. He threw her onto the bed and surveyed the room.

"This is as good a place as any," he said. "No one will come looking for you, but I think your friend's boyfriend might raise an alarm."

He ran around, throwing clothes on the floor, and knocking her laptop over. He brought his foot down on it.

"No more writing for you."

He stared at her for a reaction, but she looked back blankly. Completely numb from the shock of losing her best friend, she could no longer fully rationalize Jonas's words or actions. She could only look on as her brain sent random thoughts to cover the hostile display.

He tied Ren's hands to the bedpost with strips of cloth from one of her favorite shirts. Kai had bought it during one of their vacations.

It was a time when she'd thought he'd been hers, but she had been wrong. He had never belonged to her.

"It turns out Gonzo has a thing for women, too," he said, building a lie. "He caught you and Becky together, and it was too much for him."

The lie he was going to tell the police snapped Ren back. She pulled on her bonds, but her body was too weak to break them.

"Becky's been missing for days," Ren pointed out. "No one will believe you."

He rewarded her with a hard slap. Ren's head bounced against the headboard, but she fought to stay conscious.

Jonas paced the room, scanning his brain for another way to lead the authorities away from making him a suspect. "Fine. You kept Becky here because you were jealous of her. When Gonzo found her, he tied you up to call the police, but you killed him, and then you killed yourself."

Ren didn't have enough time to tell him that she couldn't have killed Gonzo if her hands were tied to the bed. She was horrified by the gun coming closer to her.

He took her hand, forcing the gun into it. Keeping a firm grip on her fingers, he turned the gun toward her mouth.

"We may not have as much fun as I'd planned, but I think I like this ending."

Ren closed her eyes and waited on the end. She thought about her baby and concentrated on her innocent face. Her mind went to Gonzo, and she wondered if he'd wait for her to step into the Great Beyond with him.

A loud sound cracked, and Ren cringed. She didn't feel a bullet sail through her mouth, and Jonas's body crumpled. Gonzo stood behind him with a hammer in his hand.

CHAPTER 42

Looking back at her time at the lake ripped her to the core. Ren could see the patterns she'd always known were there, but she'd never been ready to deal with the issues until she'd almost been killed.

She started with the reason she'd been in a relationship with Kai. It would take some time to sort out how much she'd ignored about his true personality. She wished she could say there weren't signs, but even before the accident, she should have questioned why an outgoing person like Kai had no real, long-term friendships.

He'd had one, but it was a secret buried in the dark with the bodies he and Jonas put in the water hole.

If she were honest, she'd made a lie out of her marriage, and Kai made it easier for her with his death. Ren continued her pregnancy, building the lie of the grieving widow who wanted to be alone. It had allowed her to keep her pregnancy and the baby's death a secret.

On the night her front bag of water had broken, she'd called Gonzo. She was scared, as she wasn't due for another month.

He drove lightning-fast to the hospital, and they waited for the doctor while Gonzo held both of her hands. It was too early for her to deliver the baby without complications, but when the doctor broke her main water bag, Ren felt relieved. Later, she hated herself for the pain it took away from the contractions, but at that moment, the water helped the baby make her way into the world.

The baby didn't cry. Despite the best efforts of the doctor and nurses, she never took a breath.

Ren held her and stared at her smooth face with rounded cheeks. The nurse showed her the baby's eyes and marked their color on a form.

Gonzo took the baby when she held her out to him, and his face crumbled. He sat on the chair beside her, crying and telling her he wished he could have saved her. Ren wished she could have helped her baby, but Lillian Bell was buried in a graveyard in the mountains where Ren planned to be buried when she died. They'd be miles away from Kai, even though the plot of land next to him had been purchased for her.

Ren had never dealt with her daughter's death, so she had made a world where she'd been happy with her husband. She didn't have to confront the trauma or the pain, but the water was always there, reminding her of her fears and heartbreak.

A detective, Landy Ball, called Ren once a week. He was a nice man, who seemed to have a slight crush on her. She used excuses to ward off his dinner invitations, but he still let her know what he could about the case.

Detective Ball informed her they'd found nine bodies in the water hole and six buried in the woods. Among them were ten girls who'd gone missing around the lake, but some of the other bodies hadn't been identified. She told him what she knew about Jonas and his family, and he relayed that Jonas's mother and two of the women his father had dated had been found in the water hole.

He spared her most of the grisly details, but he claimed the bodies seemed to go back several decades. It made Ren curious if *the collection* had started with Jonas, Riley, and her husband, or if Jonas's father had put women in that hole before he showed it to his family. Maybe it was a warning to his unfaithful wife, and she began slipping him a sedative in the afternoon to keep him from harming her. It would certainly have explained how Jonas and Riley knew where to hide their mother's dead body.

The detective told her about Jonas and his innocent pleas. They'd caught him trying to escape his house, carrying Colette's dead body with him.

Gonzo had passed out after knocking Jonas over the head. Whether from the stress or the force of Jonas falling on her, Ren blacked out. Jonas had regained consciousness faster than Gonzo and her.

Blane had called the police when Gonzo didn't respond to his calls, and they were at Ren's house within minutes.

Maybe it was the approach of the authorities that made him run away instead of making sure they were dead. Maybe Jonas's milder personality took over when he woke up and he couldn't finish the job. Ren didn't want to evaluate the reasons beyond a fleeting thought.

Even if his other personality had killed the bulk of the women in their *collection*, Jonas had practically admitted to killing Delaney and Colette. He swore he had nothing to do with the torture and murder of the women in the water hole, but he confessed to having a relationship with most of the ones they found in the woods.

Ren shuddered when she thought about her time with him. She'd been so blinded by his looks and her desires that she'd ignored the warning signs. He'd been demanding and moody, but he covered it with kindness and physical attention.

Jonas had tried to call her from jail. She hung up as soon as the disembodied voice announced that she had a call from a local correctional facility. That night, she lay awake for hours, wondering what he could have to say to her.

Gonzo had her change her phone number the next day.

They lived next to one another in cozy condos. They'd decided their homes were an emotional burden, and they sold their properties. Ren had gotten less than three-fourths of the market value for the lake house, but she had been glad to get rid of it. The home she'd shared with Kai had been sold in one weekend, and after Gonzo had retrieved a few of her items from the time before she'd met Kai, she'd had movers pack up its contents.

Everything in the house reminded her of Kai, so she added it to her storage building, promising herself she'd have the strength to go through it all one day. When she thought about the pictures of Kai and her and the gifts he'd given her, she couldn't imagine a day when she'd be willing to sort through what remained of her time with her husband.

Ren and Gonzo talked every day. They had a code of knocking on the wall that would let the other one know they were headed out to their shared garden. They hardly spoke about what had happened at the lake, but Ren had thanked her friend for saving her life.

Even though he hadn't been there when Jonas had killed Becky, Gonzo still blamed himself for her murder. Sometimes, he got a faraway look, and he'd say, "Her eyes." Ren understood his feelings, and Blane was extra supportive when Gonzo's shoulders were heavy from the weight he was holding.

The leaves had turned before Gonzo had proposed to Blane, and the two of them lived comfortably beside her. As far as she could tell, they never fought, and Blane always seemed to know when to give Gonzo some space.

Gonzo's paintings had become darker, and it was hard for him to hold a brush for long periods. His doctors told him the bullet had missed his heart and lungs and he would make a full recovery, but Ren only agreed with them in terms of the physical component. Mentally, her friend would have a deep scar very few people would understand.

His work usually featured women with shining blond hair or dead babies. The women were in a multitude of positions, but they were all dead, with large, bulging eyes. Ren was thankful when Gonzo painted other things, even when the subjects looked curiously like Jonas. One of his pieces centered on a man with dark hair and a dimple on the left side of his chin. Only his profile could be seen, as the man dipped his head to lick the blood off a knife while holding his cowboy hat in place with the other hand.

That picture had haunted her nightmares.

She'd had plenty of terrible dreams. She ran down the path between the lake houses, or up the basement steps, but Jonas always caught her. He pushed the barrel of the gun deep into her mouth and fed her the bullet he'd intended to give her.

Sometimes he haunted her during the day, too. She'd look over at the people moving on the other side of the street and catch a glimpse of him. It was enough to make her heart stop until she remembered he was locked in a jail cell.

Ren went outside to collect her mail. Gonzo was gone on a trip with Blane, and Ren had stayed indoors. She avoided the people who milled about on the sidewalk in front of her city apartment, and they ignored her as she sat on her balcony, drinking tea and thinking about her next book.

She planned to write a romance. She was already halfway through it, and she could tell she was writing the love story she wanted. She'd never find a man as wonderful as the one in her story. Even though the female protagonist irks him to no end, he's still polite and gentlemanly until he realizes he's falling in love with her. She had to send back the advance for her last nonfiction piece, but the company put her in touch with a publisher who was interested in her story idea.

On her way to the mailbox, several of the people who lived in the complex of condos waved to her. She nodded back, acknowledging their effort, but prohibiting conversation.

A man passed her and smiled. She dipped her head, blushing. She'd tried to escape the attention of the tall, dark-haired man, but he seemed to check his mail at the same time as her, even though Ren varied the times she went to the mailbox.

She opened her letterbox with a key, and he slid his key into the slot above hers. Usually, her neighbors would wait for each other, hanging back a little, and allowing the other person to move before they stepped up to the box. However, the tall man used the opportunity to get close to Ren.

She couldn't help but breathe in the rich scent of sandalwood. His fingers touched her hand as he pulled away with his mail.

"Sorry," he said, in a voice deeper than the middle of the ocean.

"It's fine." Ren kept her head bowed as she almost ran back to her door.

She didn't read the envelopes in her hand until she was inside. The letter was on top, making the mail beneath it heavier.

Even though the return address bore Jonas's name, she tore open the letter. She couldn't say what compelled her to read it, but she stood in her kitchen, devouring every word.

He started by professing his love to her, and he begged her not to testify against him. He proclaimed his innocence, insisting that Colette and the girls he'd buried in the forest had starved to death by accident because they hadn't wanted to leave his room.

He warned her against Riley, and he pleaded with her to keep her eye out for him. Jonas claimed Riley was dangerous and that he would hunt her down.

"Fat chance since *Riley* is you, and you're locked up!" Ren spoke aloud.

Something had been nagging at her, though. She couldn't put her finger on it, but Gonzo's painting of Jonas had awakened the feeling that something wasn't right.

Detective Ball had assured her they were looking for Riley, but he hadn't had a digital footprint for over three years. Ren supposed

Riley could have been paying for his lodging and meals with cash, or he could have found a woman who was interested in keeping him up, but she doubted it. *Could Riley have been one of the bodies in the water hole?*

She texted some pleasantries to Detective Ball, and after she declined a date, she asked him if Riley could be among the dead people found around the property. He quickly responded that the only bodies they had recovered were women.

Ren went to bed early, but she couldn't sleep. Images of the lake house and Jonas kept tumbling through her mind. She gave up on sleep and poured herself a bottle of wine. She hoped it would make her as tired as it did when she was at the lake.

She stopped before she took a sip. Kai had incapacitated her with wine. Jonas's mother had done the same to their father, and she'd fallen for the same trick when Jonas had been sleeping with her.

Ren hadn't felt so inebriated by wine until she'd been at the lake house. In fact, Jonas kept bringing over bottles after the first one they'd shared.

A soft scratching jolted her out of her thoughts, and she ran to the window in the kitchen. She'd been right about the source of the noise, as a leaf brushed against the pane. She turned the lock on it, wondering when she'd last opened it.

Jonas had been good to her, telling her exactly what she'd wanted to hear, except for the first night he'd brought over the wine. It was the first time she'd noticed that he put his hair into two styles. It had been combed to the side, and she'd been entranced by the dimple on the left side of his chin.

Ren had to stop and grab onto the table. She recalled the family picture she'd seen before Jonas had carried her into his room. The two boys in the picture had dimples, but they were mirror images of each other.

Jonas's dimple had been on the right side of his mouth. She had seen it many times when they were out together or sharing an intimate moment, but the man who had brought Ren the bottle of wine had a dimple on the left side of his chin.

There were a lot of things Jonas could have done to make himself look more like Riley. Ren had thought that he'd assumed an alter ego when he'd donned tennis shoes and parted his hair to the side, but he couldn't have faked the dimple.

She raced for her phone, ready to call Detective Ball and let him know a killer was on the loose, but her phone wasn't where she left it. It beeped behind her, and even though she'd never expected to see him again, she knew Riley was there.

He had never been Jonas's other personality. He had been the monster chasing her in her dreams who had killed most of the women they'd found on his and her properties.

Could he have had enough time to have escaped before she and Gonzo regained consciousness? So many things about that night were still hazy, but he hadn't been in her bedroom when she woke, so she was certain he had done it.

Riley had been the one to press the gun into her mouth. Even though Jonas was guilty of his own crimes, his brother deserved to be rotting away in a cell next to him.

The familiarity with which Riley moved showed he'd been present long before that moment. He had been waiting for her to discover the open window, so he could play another one of his vicious games.

She was unable to move, frozen with fear and the suddenness of his appearance. She could hardly breathe when she saw the sharp blade of the knife.

"Hey, Lauren," he said, stepping up behind her and bringing to mind the name her husband had given her. He lifted the hair from her shoulders and kissed her neck. "You're going to be the first trophy in my new collection."

The End

Did you like the story?

If you enjoyed the story, please consider leaving a review on retailer sites. Every positive reader comment makes the book more visible to other readers.

Thank you for reading The Tears in the Water!

Jonas's Watergate Salad

General Foods' "Pistachio Pineapple Delight" was renamed in 1975. For anyone who has studied Richard Nixon's presidency, "Watergate" is a symbol of betrayal. This is Jonas's recipe, so you can draw all the parallels.

Ingredients

- 1 small package of instant pistachio pudding mix

- 1 (eight-ounce) can of crushed pineapple, with juice

- 1 cup of miniature marshmallows

- 4 ounces of whipped topping

Directions

1. Combine the crushed pineapple without draining the juice,

instant pudding mix, and mini marshmallows in a large bowl. Mix.

2. Fold in the whipped topping.

3. Chill for two hours before serving. Enjoy!

Acknowledgments

My mama passed away, but not before she read this book. She loved it and tried to figure out the ending before she got to it. I'm glad to say, I kept my mama, an avid and perceptive reader, stumped. Her words were: *"Wow. That was a heck of an ending. Tears in the Water is a real rollercoaster of a ride. Great read and great job Courtnee Serene."*

Now, does that mean anything to the average reader? Probably not. But the average reader would understand my happiness when they realized my mama devoured almost a book a day and read for sixty-five years of her life. My mama's message made my day!

Thank you, Mama, for reading my work. I wrote thrillers for you, and as you drifted away on our last phone call, I told you I needed you to live so I could write more stories for you. I could almost hear you encouraging me to write, even if you were gone. I'll do my best to honor your memory.

Tosha is my main supporter and my favorite fan. My sweet daughter deserves more than just a mention. She designed and maintains my website, www.courtneeturnerhoyle.com. If you've shopped on the site, read my blogs or recipes, or watched my interviews, you've looked at the hours she's poured into the construction.

Thank you, Tosha, for your help. I have enjoyed talking to you as we discuss each chapter, and I'm sorry, but I will not tell if Ren lived or died. You'll have to use your imagination.

Stereling, I hope you read this story. I think you'll enjoy most of it.

Legacee, this is your birthday book! You should definitely read this one. I hope it's strange and creepy enough to do justice to your special day.

Journee, Jubilee, Legende, and Rynegade, you are loved and treasured. You can read this book when you're older, and I hope you make better decisions than the characters.

Thank you, Debbie, for reading my work. You saw a sad eleven-year-old, and you gave her your attention and helped her believe in herself.

Thank you, Sweet 15 Designs. As always, the cover is beautiful, and I appreciate your attention to detail.

Lisa, you were the inspiration for Gonzo and every other straight-forward best friend in my books. Thank you for "sock hand" and telling me to grow my bangs out.

I appreciate Linda, Elaine, Lisa, Tammy, and Judy for their support. Your words mean more to me than you'll ever know.

Thank you, my friends in the written world. I hope you continue to read my work and tell me your thoughts in reviews and messages on my website.

About the Author

Courtnee Turner Hoyle is a travel agent, mom, multi-genre writer, and an award-winning author of the books in the Pale Woods Mystery Series, It's About Time Series, and Rasputin's Dynasty Trilogy, in addition to several stand-alone novels and a few short stories that have been anthologized. The first book in her Pale Woods Mystery Series, My Brother's Keeper, has won five awards. The culture and views of her Tennessee home have forced her to find her own perspective. While she may embrace the traditions of her area, she has set non-negotiable boundaries, especially against sweet tea, chocolate, and unannounced visitors. Courtnee graduated from East Tennessee State University with multiple undergraduate degrees and a master's degree and developed unique ways of dividing the personalities of the people in her life to create quirky, relatable characters. She encourages you to write splendid reviews of her books on any retailer site and share them on social media. Good reviews from her readers make her jump up and down in her kitchen and spin her children around happily. Courtnee lives with her spirited children, braving the adventures of homeschooling, physical activity, and toddler witticisms, and believes there is a story in every experience.

Learn more about Courtnee, her hometown adventures, and her books by visiting www.courtneeturnerhoyle.com or by plucking the leaves of her Link Tree (linktr.ee/Courtnee_).

Also By Courtnee

Hollis's Hobby
By Courtnee Turner Hoyle
Do you trust your lover?
After an abusive childhood and soul-splitting heartbreak, Hollis hovers around her hometown, secretly killing the men who are unfortunate enough to fall for her charms, until her lonely friend, Josie, asks Hollis to move in with her. Hollis attempts to drop "Holli", the alter ego who dispatches her unsuspecting lovers, but she finds it difficult to function as a teacher when she sees the evidence of abuse on a student. To veer away from her murderous path, Hollis forms a relationship with the father of one of her students, Quillen, but he's running from a secret Hollis may not understand. Hollis's sad and twisted past has never been unearthed, but will Quillen's influence cause her to dig up details that could risk her capture? When all Hollis's secrets threaten to come to the surface, will she continue to live under the guise she's created, or will Hollis's hobby be revealed?

HOLLIS'S
HOBBY
COURTNEE TURNER HOYLE

Also By Courtnee

Solomon's Tears
By Courtnee Turner Hoyle

Are the ghosts in her house or in her mind?
Ketron Gouge is puzzled when she feels like one of her children is missing. A quick check calms her panicked mind, but the uncomfortable thought continues to concern her.
Ketron and her husband, Marvin, bought a home they hoped would be perfect for their growing family. Soon, however, Marvin develops a drinking problem and Ketron becomes more anxious about the mysterious shadows and disembodied crying in the house. Most of her five children seem to be conscious of the uncanny events, giving credence to Ketron's worries, but her best friend and therapist think it may be a product of her overstressed mind.
Ghosts from her past and memories of her childhood tumble to the surface, reminding her of her mentally unstable mother, and wonders if there's truth to the nagging idea that someone is missing.

And when she sees things in her house, she thinks it may be time to accept an inescapable truth.

Also By Courtnee

This spine-tingling coloring book is the perfect way to get you in the mood for the spooky season—no matter the time of year! Get your creative juices flowing as you explore the dark and mysterious Pale Woods, where Courtnee Turner Hoyle's incredible imagination comes alive. As you wander through the woods, you'll explore strange and otherworldly homes that remain on the edge of nightmares, and each page will challenge you to think of new and exciting ways to bring them to life.

This complement to Courtnee Turner Hoyle's Pale Woods Series is complete with forty pages of images. Prepare for the Halloween season, or get your creepy organ music ready and cue the thunderstorms.

PALE
WOODS
HAUNTED HOUSES